THE GOOD ONES

LaWanda Butler

The Good Ones
Copyright © 2013 by LaWanda Butler

ISBN: 978-1-7321200-0-6 (Print Edition)

ISBN: 978-1-7321200-1-3 (eBook Edition)

Contents

It's early in the morning, and everyone is still in bed in a quiet suburban neighborhood. One of the neighborhood houses has two cars in the driveway, two trees—one in the front yard and one in the back—and a flower bed out front. Inside the house all seems quiet; the couple is in bed asleep in the master bedroom. Mark is an attractive twenty-six-year-old with a fit body, short brown hair, and green eyes. Sleeping next to Mark is Debbie, his wife; she is twenty-five years old, in shape, and attractive, with long blond hair and blue eyes.

Mark is tossing and turning in bed. He is having a nightmare, dreaming about when he was younger, about seven years old. Mark's parents were part of a bank-robbing gang. The gang lived together in an abandoned warehouse. In his nightmare, Mark sees himself watching the grownups count money from their big score. He sees himself playing with all the other gangster kids. One is a little girl, Sonya; she was around five, African American, with big brown eyes. Mark never had any siblings, but he always treated Sonya as if she were his little sister; he would make sure she had something to eat and that she had a blanket when it was time to sleep.

One day, when everyone was getting ready to eat, the police came rushing in. All of the adults were killed, except Sonya's mother, Teresa. Teresa grabbed Sonya and went running out of the building. In his nightmare, Mark is chasing after Teresa, reaching out and calling her name.

"Sonya! Sonya!"

Sonya is screaming back at him, "Mark! Mark!"

And then she is gone, but he can still hear her voice lingering, calling to him.

"Mark?" she says calmly. He can't understand it. Sonya isn't screaming anymore; she sounds a little different.

"Sonya, is that you?" he asks.

Sonya repeats his name again, except now he can hear what sounds like Debbie's voice in the mix. "Mark! Mark, come on, honey, wake up. *Mark*!"

Mark awakens from his nightmare and sees Debbie. "Oh, hi, honey. Was I doing it again?"

"Yes!"

"Sorry about that. I don't know why I started dreaming about Sonya again," he tells her, fully awake now.

"That's okay, baby. I'm just glad you told me who Sonya was so that I could stop thinking you were dreaming about another woman."

Now the smart thing for Mark to do would be to just agree with his wife and say nothing else, but Mark has a habit of sometimes being sarcastic at the wrong moments, and this is one of those times.

"I'm glad too. It has made things around here a lot easier."

Debbie stares at him. "What?"

Mark, realizing his mistake, tries to play it off. "Oh, nothing, baby. I was just trying to be funny, you know."

"Uh-huh," Debbie replies, a bit of attitude in her voice. "So, do you have time for a long breakfast this morning, or will it be your usual—just coffee?"

"Just coffee, thanks."

After Debbie has left the room, Mark gets out of bed slowly and goes into the bathroom. Mark looks at himself in the mirror, and flexes his muscle. "Yep, I still got it." He gives himself a wink and then gets into the shower.

The Past

Mark is daydreaming while showering and begins talking to himself. "I wonder whether Sonya is okay."

Mark thinks back to when he was a twenty four year old cop in the police file room, which is as big as a library. There are files on the shelves and in file cabinets. He sees the clerk, Gina who acts like a mother to him, is sitting behind a desk, like a librarian. She looks up at Mark and smiles. She has dark brown glasses and is a little on the thick side, but she is sweet.

"Don't worry, Mark. We'll find something, why don't you let your fellow officer help you?" she says.

He nods in agreement. Then Mark tells Gina it's not about telling about finding Sonya they are helping, but he believes it might be more than that so he's letting them help with only half in case they run into some information on anyone at the station. They both look through the files.

Flipping pages, he looks over at the clerk, excited.

"I take it you found something?" the clerk says.

"Yeah!" Mark replies. "I found out that the gang robbed the wrong people and that my parents and the other gang members had a hit put on them."

"Oh my," Gina says. "Does it tell you anything else?"

"Nope," Mark replies.

"So, what have you learned since starting this investigation?" she asks.

"Well, it hasn't been easy; I had to dig deep. I discovered things about the precinct that they would have preferred to keep buried," he says. "For one thing, I discovered that the cops who showed up were dirty and on the payroll of the Scar Backs."

"The Scar Backs?" she asks. "Aren't they one of the most notorious gangs out there?"

"Yes."

"Did you find out anything about this Sonya girl?" she asks.

"No," Mark answers. "I think the information about her is in sealed files, which I don't have access to."

"Sealed files, huh?" Gina gets up and leaves the room, then returns a few minutes later. Leaning toward Mark, she pitches her voice low and says, "Listen, I could lose my job."

"Don't worry, I won't tell a soul," Mark says.

"All right. Follow me."

Mark nods and follows her to a door in the back. Gina looks around, unlocks the door, and they enter the room. She locks the door behind them. "Now," she says, "only certain captains and above have access to the files on this computer, and even they have to have permission from the IA first. In case you're wondering whether our captain has permission, he does not. They monitor these files all the time.

"We can take a look while Internal Affairs is updating their monitor server, which is every Wednesday at five am for three minutes. So since it is Wednesday, and it will be five am in five minutes, we can look safely without getting caught by the computer security—at least as long as we use this computer."

"Two questions," Mark says. "First, how did you get this info about IA? Second, if we can do this during their update times, why can't we just use any computer?"

"Mark," she says, smiling, "sometimes a woman is out drinking with her friend, who is a record clerk at IA, and sometimes he lets things slip because he is drunk."

Mark is amused by the revelation.

Gina informs him that if they use any other computer, they will be caught immediately, but if they use *this* computer, which is one of IA's, the chances of them getting caught are slim. IA will just think it's one of the authorized people using it. Of course, she makes sure he understands that they keep records of what files are looked at and when they are viewed.

"If we play our cards right," she says, "we can look at the files real quick and get out before they know we're in the system. Are you ready to do this?"

"Yes," Mark replies.

"Good. Now, as far as I know, nobody is scheduled to use this computer, but we should be ready to shutdown if somebody comes."She looks at her watch and turns on the computer. Once it is booted up, she types in the password when prompted, and the computer grants them access. They begin looking at files and find one labeled "SCAR BACKS." Opening the file, both Gina and Mark read quickly. She pulls up two files at a time, reading one while Mark reads the other.

"Two minutes," she says.

Mark starts reading faster, and hits pay dirt with one of the files; they both keep reading quickly, and then Gina's watch starts to beep. She closes the files, and before she can shut down the computer they hear footsteps coming down the hall. She continues to shut down the computer while Mark runs over and turns off the lights.

"Let's get out of here," she tells Mark. He's thinking the same thing.

"Do you know another way out?" he whispers."It sounds like someone is outside the door."

"No," she whispers back."There is no other way out."

Mark's heart drops when he hears the door knob turn. They both hide quickly behind the shelves before the door opens and a man comes in. He turns on the lights and sits down at the computer. He is about to turn it on when his cell phone rings.

"Todd Smith here," he answers.

Mark is unfamiliar with the man, but when he looks over at Gina he can see pure terror in her eyes. The way she's looking at him, it seems like she's afraid of not only losing her job, but also losing her life.

Mark grabs her hand to reassure her that he will get them out of there safely. They both continue to watch Todd as he talks on his cell. Todd gets up and starts walking around as he talks. Mark and Gina move to stay out of his line of sight as he is pacing around. Todd begins to move closer to them, and they realize that they are trapped. Right before Todd gets to them, Mark motions for Gina to get under a wide office desk by the wall with him.

Todd walks to where they just were and looks around like something is wrong. Todd then heads back over to the computer and turns it on and ends his conversation on the phone. He starts looking at files on the computer while Mark and Gina are still trapped under the desk. Once Todd is finished, he turns off the computer and gets up, and then leaves the room turning the lights off as he goes. Mark and Gina breathe a sigh of relief and are about to crawl out from their hiding place when the room's door comes flying open.

They freeze under the desk as Todd comes back in the room. He walks over to the computer, gets the cell phone he'd forgotten, and leaves. Mark and Gina wait five minutes before they move from under the desk.

"Let me check to make sure he is gone," Mark whispers. She nods and when Mark says the coast is clear, they head to her private office.

Mark looks around; it's just a hole in the wall—nothing more than a small room with enough space for a desk and chair. She has tried to fix it up with posters of different locations, but he can tell it isn't the best space for an office. Mark can see that she is still shaken by what just happened.

"Don't worry, he didn't see us. We will be okay," he says.

Gina sits down at her desk and tries to catch her breath. "I have never been so afraid in my life. Are you sure he didn't see us?"

"I'm sure," Mark replies. "Listen, if you're still scared, I'll check around and make sure he didn't see anything. And I would stay away from your friend for awhile, just in case."

"All right. Well, back to business. So, according to what I read, the Scar Backs gang did not care about the kids enough to have them killed."

"Interesting," Mark replies. "Anything else?"

"Yes, it also said Sonya's mom took her to use as a bargaining chip. Apparently, she thought that Mickey the leader of the Scar Backs must have a soft spot for kids, and she could use that to save her life."

"I see. What a desperate move."

"I agree," Gina says. "Did you see anything that said what happened after she escaped?"

"Yes," Mark answers. "According to an informant, things did not go off quite as she had planned."

The records clerk looks at Mark, intrigued. Mark tells her what he found out. "According to the informant, when Teresa arrived at Mickey's office things seemed all right." Mark remembers what the file had said, and can picture what happened almost twenty years ago, when Sonya's mom went into Mickey's office that day…

Sonya's mom walks into Mickey's office—a large, luxurious office with a big desk and chair, bookshelves, and paintings on the wall—and sees Mickey, a man in his early thirties, sitting behind his desk. His two assistants, Gossip (late twenties) and Kiss-Up (early thirties), are standing on either side of him. "Sorry, Mickey," Teresa explains, "we had no idea that place was one of yours. To make up for my mistake,

I offer you my daughter. Do with her as you will; just please, spare my life."

Mickey looks at Teresa with no emotion; she cannot tell what he is thinking. Mickey replies, "Fine, I'll take her, but not to do what you're thinking. I'm not a pedophile; she will work and learn the business. My wife has been very depressed since we lost our daughter, and I'm sure your daughter feels the same way, since she lost her mother."

Teresa looks at Mickey, confused. "What do you mean? I'm standing right here."

Mickey smiles at her, making her feel like all is well. "Not for long. Goodbye, Teresa!"

Mickey points a gun straight at Teresa's head—bang! Sonya is standing next to her mom when she gets shot. Mickey laughs. Blood splatters on Sonya's face and clothes. Teresa's body falls back while she is still holding Sonya's hand. Sonya, seeing her mother shot and then falling down dead, begins to cry.

Mark finishes telling the records clerk what he'd learned from the file and says, "Basically, that is the last they wrote about what happened to Sonya and her mother."

"So…what about the dirty cops?"Gina asks.

Mark replies, "They're dead, so the trail has gone cold. Mickey probably had his personal hit man Assassin or Assassin's men kill them."

"Do you think Sonya is safe?"

"Yes," Mark answers. "I know she is." Mark starts thinking about two years earlier to the day he found out who Sonya was with. Jake a fellow cop had told him. That was when they had been friends. Jake told Mark that Sonya was with the Scar Backs, and if he wanted anymore information he should go see Manny.

"Who is Manny?" Mark had asked Jake.

"He's one of the informants we used to use, until he tested dirty for drugs. He still has some information, and you can use him off the record, especially since this is your own personal investigation," Jake replies.

"Great! Where can I find him?" asks Mark.

"He moves around a lot, but there is a club on 9th Street where he likes to hang out. You might start there," Jake says.

Jake starts to head back to his desk when Mark asks him if Manny's picture will be in the records room with the rest of the informants. Jake tells Mark yes, and Mark heads to the record room. Mark starts looking through the informant records. There are only a select few informants who are not in the record room, and that is for their safety. The police cannot have it written down, in case someone gets access to it. But these guys are not in danger like that.

Mark looks in the M files. "Okay, Manny, Manny, Manny. Hmm, that is strange. He isn't here."

He walks over to the old records clerk, Dave, a man with a shady demeanor. "Excuse me. I can't seem to find a certain file, are there any files checked out?"

"Nope. Every file you want is right there," Dave answered. "Can I help you find anyone in particular?"

Mark tells him he is looking for the file on Manny. Dave tells him that the file was destroyed this morning, since Manny is no longer a reliable source.

"Oh, I see," Mark says. "Well, thanks for the info."

Mark leaves the record room, but he finds it strange that Jake wouldn't have mentioned the file was going to be destroyed. Mark goes to Jake's desk to ask him, but finds out Jake is off on a drug raid. Mark decides to go to the club on 9th Street, like Jake had said, and start there. When Mark arrives at the club, the parking lot is deserted.

"Well, it must only be open at night," he says to himself. He decides to return later, but just before he walks away, he notices a "Gone Out Of Business" sign on the door.

Mark peeks inside the window and can see that the building is empty, and judging by the level of dust, he guesses it has been empty for months. Mark can't understand why Jake would tell him to come to a place that is closed. Mark starts to walk to his car when a homeless man comes up to him and asks him for change.

"Spare a dollar, sir?"

Mark looks the man over. "What's your name?"

"Lucas," the man responds.

"Well, Lucas, I'll give you this dollar if you can tell me where I might find a man call Manny."

The man nods and smiles, and then points to under the bridge across the street. Mark thanks the man and gives him the dollar before walking cautiously across the street and under the bridge.

When Mark gets there, at first he sees nothing. But then he spots a man sleeping in a box by the bridge. Mark stays cautious as he wakes the man up. He has a strong body odor and bad breath, and Mark has to put his hand over his nose to deaden the overpowering smell.

"Wh…what? What do you want?" says the man.

"Manny?" replies Mark.

"It's been awhile since my services have been called upon. You must be a cop. I'm right, aren't I?"

"Yes."

"Hot dog! I knew it—you guys need me again. So what can I do for you?" Manny asks.

"I was wondering if you could give me some information about Sonya, Mickey's adopted daughter."

Manny thinks a bit, then answers, "Sure I can, and can I get some food if I help you?"

"Sure," Mark says.

"Great! I can tell you that she is just fine for now; he has no intentions of killing her. She and his other children are out of town."

Mark looks at Manny, puzzled. "When you said for now, what do you mean?"

"Well, you know how Mickey is. He can change his mind at the drop of a hat. He is known to do that kind of stuff. So what's your name?"

"I see, Mark" Mark replies.

"Well glad to meet you Mark. Do you still want me to continue the investigation, that other cop had me on?" Manny asks.

Mark doesn't know what he is talking about. "Sure, but why don't you tell me about it," he says.

"The other cop wanted me to check out a contact that Mickey has on the inside," Manny says.

"Oh yes. Of course," Mark replies.

"I'll leave the information in the usual spot inside the night club," said Manny.

"Okay. How will I get inside?" Mark asks.

"The door in the back. Lock is broke, so you should be able to get in that way," Manny replies.

"All right, see you tomorrow," Mark tells him, then watches as Manny goes off across the street and disappears around the corner. Mark heads back to his car and leaves to go back to the station.

The next day, Mark goes to the night club on 9th Street but he finds nothing inside. Mark starts to look for Manny and runs into the same homeless man, Lucas, from before. He asks him where Manny is. Lucas tells him that Manny is in the river under the bridge. Mark calls for backup and goes to the bridge where Manny was sleeping. He can see blood inside of his box. He looks over at the shallow river that runs under the bridge, and there is Manny body lying in the middle of it. Mark doesn't know what happened, but the other cop Manny was working for might. Backup arrives and covers the scene. Mark sees Jake and goes over to talk to him.

"Hey. Can I ask you something?"

"Sure," Jake replies.

"Do you know who Manny was working for down at the station?" Mark asks.

"Yeah, I forgot all this people were before you got hire he was working for Cliff. But that ended when he died ten months ago. Why do you ask?"

"Oh nothing, Manny was just talking crazy. How did Cliff die?" Mark asks.

"Heart attack," Jake says.

Mark tells Jake he is sad to hear about that, and that he wished he could have met Cliff. Mark decided he'd have to find out more about this after he finished up all his other cases.

* * *

Mark snaps out of his daydream. Mark tells Gina "I found an old informant the cops used to use, and he told me she is safe and out of town. As far as he knows, Mickey has no intentions of killing her."

"Well, that's good," replies the clerk. "Have you thought of a way to get her out?"

"Yeah, I've thought of a way, but mostly everybody would get killed in that scenario. It's hard to get into that group and then come out of it without getting killed," Mark says. "I have a plan now that I believe will work, but it will take years and years."

"What is it?" she asks.

"Well, I hope that we can find some evidence big enough to hold Mickey in prison for the rest of his life," replies Mark.

"I see. Hasn't anyone tried this before?" she asks.

Mark replies, "Yes, but somehow his lawyer always gets him off. What happens is, evidence and witnesses will disappear without a trace. I mean, if I can figure out how the drugs disappear out of the evidence room and witnesses to Mickey's crimes just disappear off of the face of the earth I bet I could get him put in prison for the rest of his life. I've tried, but have gotten nowhere. Whoever he's got that is covering up things for him is good and obviously dangerous. I think we should meet in your office again to discuss any new information you have."

"Are you sure that is safe since whoever he has is so dangerous and it could be anyone we can't meet in my office. So how and where will we meet and talk without anyone catching on, since the person could be watching us?"

Mark thinks for a moment then says, "If you ever want to meet with me and you think it's not safe to talk, just say 'How's Cleo doing?' "

"All right. Where should we meet?" Gina asks.

"Well, we can meet at the dollar theatre on 15th Street. Just mention things that are in the movie so I'll know without a doubt which movie. As for the time, make it sound like you're talking about money. You might say something like, I have two hundred and thirty dollars. Which tells me it's the two-thirty showing of that film."

She nods in understanding. The clerk tells Mark not to worry and that at some point, he will find a way to get Sonya back safely.

The Good

Mark is lost in his thoughts, talking to himself in his head. *The day is finally here; we are finally going to get this guy for good.* Mark is still just standing in the shower, lost in thought, when Debbie pops her head in through the curtain. "Mark, you are going to be late, baby."

Mark snaps out of his daydreaming and rushes to get dressed. He takes his coffee, kisses Debbie goodbye, and leaves for work. Mark arrives at the police station and hurries into the conference room.

Captain Jeff is in front of everyone, getting ready to speak. Mark sees Jake sitting next to Tim. Jerome and Sheila are sitting together; Jerome motions to Mark to sit with them. Jeff begins talking.

"There has been a string of criminal activity lately. I believe the Scar Backs might be behind this, but we will need to get proof before we can act. Once we have the proof we need, we can come up with a plan to take them down."

All the cops listen intently. Jake raises his hand, and Jeff acknowledges him.

"Captain, I have a couple of leads that I need to check out. They might be able to give us the information we are looking for."

"That's fine," the captain replies. "Everyone, I want you to check out all leads you have. Leave no stone unturned; check everything, from their drug activities to their blackmail activities, no matter how crazy or insignificant it may seem. I want it found."

The Bad

At the same time the cops are having their meeting, another meeting is taking place in another conference room. The Scar Backs have gathered together for a meeting, discussing the plans for a big shipment of drugs that is supposed to arrive. The gang is sitting around a conference table: Mickey, Kiss-Up, Bone Breaker, Killer, Crazy, Money, Bullseye, Informer, and Eric. Mickey is talking to them.

"Police activity has been on the rise lately, and we have some trusted guys who are keeping us informed. I think we just need to create a diversion for the police so we can handle our business when the drugs come in on Friday. We'll have the informer guys tell us if our diversion is working on them or not."

Bullseye asks, "Sounds like a plan, Boss, but what kind of diversion should we create?"

Mickey looks at Bullseye, a little annoyed, and then replies, "Easy. We'll have a big-time bank robbery over at the Metro Bank."

"Won't the police wonder why we are robbing a bank?" Bullseye asks. "I mean, sorry, Boss, for sounding like I'm questioning your judgment here, but won't they?"

Mickey gives him an insincere smile and replies, "That is quite all right; I'm glad to see that you are on your toes. We won't actually be robbing it ourselves; we'll send one of our little peon gangs down there to rob it."

Bullseye replies, "I see."

"I'm glad that you do. While the police are busy with that, we will receive our shipment without hassle."

"Brilliant, Boss, "Kiss-Up responds. Bone Breaker, Crazy, Money, Informer, Bullseye, and Eric join Kiss-Up in telling Mickey how great his plan is.

"Yeah, great plan," says Money.

"Yeah, yeah," Mickey says."Now get out of here." He watches as the guys leave. He grabs Bullseye's arm just before he leaves and asks, "Can I talk to you for a minute?"

"Of course," Bullseye says.

Mickey says, "I just wanted to let you know something. If you ever question me like that again, you are going to find yourself dead. Do I make myself clear?"

"Crystal," Bullseye answers.

"Good. Now, leave my sight before I change my mind and kill you!"

"Yes, Boss," Bullseye replies, and hurries out.

The Investigation

Sixteen hours later at the police precinct in Captain Jeff's office, Mark and his colleagues are all meeting with Jeff to go over all the evidence they have gathered.

"What have you all found?" Jeff asks.

Jake replies, "Well, I've got a guy on the inside. He's been there for awhile now, and he says that the big boss, Mickey, called all of the guys together for a big meeting today. He says he will find out what it is about and then let us know."

Jeff replies, "Great! Anyone else got anything?"

Jerome raises his hand and tells everyone that he has heard from a reliable source that one of the smaller gangs is getting ready for a big bank robbery this Friday. Everyone is impressed by this information.

Jeff asks, "Does your guy have any idea which bank?"

"No, I'm afraid not, but they are checking into that," Jerome replies. "Captain, also, from what I have heard, Mickey's wife and kids are back in town."

Mark grabs Jerome's arm and looks at him intently. "Jerome, are you serious?"

Jerome replies, "Yes. I thought you would like that info." He smiles at Mark. All the guys look at each other and smile.

Jeff holds his hand up for everybody to be quiet. "Okay, guys, stay focused. We have a job to do. Dismissed." Everyone leaves Jeff's office.

Outside, Mark stops Jerome. "Can I speak to you for a minute?"

They walk over by the window to talk. Mark says, "Jerome, I was wondering if you can find something out for me."

"Sure, let me guess—you want me to find out if Sonya is still with them?" Jerome asks.

"Yes," he replies, feeling grateful. "That would be great."

Jerome answers, "Well, Mark. I've been your friend since the academy. I'll do what I can to help you out."

"Great, just call me as soon as you have something," says Mark.

Jerome puts his hand on Mark's shoulder. "Sure. Can I ask you a question?"

"Sure," Mark replies.

"Why didn't you just ask Jake to find this information out for you?" he asks.

"You know why I can't. Since he did what he did to me" Mark wouldn't say it, but Jerome knew this was about Jake trying to steal his wife.

"I know, I know—he was your wife's old boyfriend."

Mark's tone betrays some annoyance. "Exactly. I don't want him causing trouble," he says, looking at Jerome as if to say, *If you press this issue any further, I'm going to kick your butt.* So Jerome drops it and tells Mark that he will have his guys check into the information Mark wants about Sonya personally. Mark thanks him, and Jerome gives him a warning.

"I hope you are prepared for the fact that she could be unreachable."

"Yeah, but—"

Jerome interrupts him. "Yeah, but…nothing. It has been too long, and she is no longer a child."

Mark replies, "I know, but I've got to try." Jerome heads to his desk, and Mark is preparing to do the same when Jeff pops his head out of his office and asks Mark to join him. Mark heads towards Jeff's office. He looks at Jerome before he goes inside.

"Do you have any idea why he would want to see me?" Mark asks.

Jerome shrugs, and tells Mark, "Good luck." Mark enters Jeff's office and closes the door.

"Jerome is right," Jeff says. "It has been a long time. Are you prepared for the fact that she may be unreachable?"

Mark looks at Jeff, surprised. "How did you know what we were talking about?"

Jeff responds, "Well, I can read lips, plus you were talking next to the vent outside my office, so I could hear every word you guys were saying." Jeff then gets the conversation back on track and asks Mark to answer the question. Mark tells Jeff that he is prepared for that, but he hopes it doesn't go in that direction.

Jeff nods. "Good to hear that you're ready. I just don't need you flaking out on us; this mission is way too important and dangerous."

"I understand, sir," Mark says before he gets up to leave.

"One more thing we need to talk about," Jeff says. Mark sits back down. "We need to talk about Jake."

"Why? That is over with."

"Apparently not. Like I just told you, I could hear you and Jerome talking. So why don't you tell me everything?" Mark says "I don't understand what you means?"

Jeff replies "Mark stop playing I just told you that I was able to hear you and Jerome talking. Now tell me everything."

"It's too embarrassing," Mark says.

Jeff replies, "Look, Mark, if you are having a problem with this guy, I need to know. The reason is…if you cannot even talk to Jake about this, then it is a problem. You know we're on a life-or-death mission."

"Yeah, but—"

Jeff interrupts. "Yeah, but nothing. Cops need to be able to trust each other. We need to know that our partners will have our backs."

"I know," Mark says.

"Yes, Mark, you do know, but you still don't trust Jake; so not only are you putting your life at risk, but you're putting everyone else's life at risk, too." Mark doesn't respond to Jeff's comments.

Jeff continues, "Mark, I can't let you be silent about this. These other cops' lives are in my hands. So out with it."

Mark tells Jeff how his wife liked to date cops and had dated guys from this precinct. Jeff looks at Mark, puzzled.

Jeff says something aloud, not really talking to Mark but more to himself. "How did I not see this where was I at?"

"Sir," Mark says, snapping Jeff to attention. Mark continues on. "The problem is that Jake tried to steal her from me on our wedding day."

"I see," Jeff says, looking shocked.

"So you can see why I don't trust him."

Jeff takes a deep breath before responding. "Yes, I can—but, Mark, you have to remember that you won; she chose you, not him."

"I know, but—"

Jeff interrupts him again. "But nothing. It is very clear; get over it, and move on. As long as you are not hiding anything from your wife, your marriage will be safe."

Mark nods, but his face betrays the fact that he does not fully believe it.

Jeff tells him, "Look, I can see that this is going to be hard for you. If you would like some reassurances, just ask Cindy. She can tell you he has moved on. You know they are dating now."

Mark replies, "Thanks, sir. I needed that."

Jeff smiles. "You're welcome. Now, get out of my office."

Mark laughs and leaves to go back to his desk.

Sonya

A fit twenty-four-year-old black female with long black hair walks toward Mickey's office. She is dressed in a sleeveless and backless shirt, and form-fitting jeans. She has a big S-shaped, zipper-like scar running down her back that shows through the back of the shirt. The woman opens the door to Mickey's office and goes in. She greets Mickey, and he looks at her and smiles.

"Ah, Sonya. So glad you could come," he says.

"Hi, Dad. The boys have just informed me of what is going on. Do you want me to pick the group that is going to rob the bank?"

Mickey responds gruffly, "No! I will handle that. I want you to help oversee the drug shipment. You are my eyes and ears. Sonya, you know you are the only one I can trust to give me the true report about what is happening." Mickey turns and looks out the window. "I don't know if this plan is going to work, but it will answer a few questions I have."

Sonya looks at Mickey with a confused expression. "Questions? What questions?"

Mickey turns back to her and smiles, with a sinister look in his eyes. "You will see soon enough."

Sonya looks at Mickey curiously, but she knows that she dare not press him for the answer. He gets up out of his seat and tells Sonya they had better get going, as they are meeting the rest of the family for lunch. Sonya agrees, and they leave the office.

A Little Romance

Later on that night, at Mark's house, Debbie has just arrived home from work at the hospital, where she is a nurse. She looks at the clock in her car; it says 6:00. Debbie sees Mark's car is already in the driveway. She smiles, gets out of the car, and walks into the house. Debbie can see that dinner has been made and is sitting on the table, waiting for her. She walks into the kitchen and sees Mark finishing cooking desert.

"What is this?" she asks.

"Dinner," Mark replies.

"I know, but usually you don't make dinner," she says.

Mark smiles and touches her face gently. "I know. I just thought that…since I'm going to be going on a dangerous mission soon, it would be a good night to talk about our future plans that you have been trying to get me to talk about for the last month. I thought it would only be right that I make dinner for you, this time, to show you that what you say does matter to me." They look at each other lovingly for a moment.

"All right, then, I'll go and take a quick shower and come right back," Debbie says.

Mark nods, and she heads toward the bathroom upstairs. A few minutes later, Mark pops his head into the shower. "I figured I would join you," he says.

Debbie smiles at him. He gets undressed and joins her in the shower. They start kissing, but then Debbie stops Mark. "Wait! What about dinner?"

Mark caresses her face and replies, "Well, I figure we could start with dessert first, because that's the best part of the meal anyway."

They start kissing again and move from the shower to the bedroom, where they move to the bed and make love. After they have finished having sex, they are lying in bed, cuddling. Debbie looks at Mark. "So, I guess now is a good time as any to talk about our future plans," she says.

Mark looks confused. "Are you sure you want to do this right now, at this moment?"

"What do you mean, at this moment?" Debbie looks at Mark like she doesn't understand his meaning.

Mark sighs and says, "Well, I thought maybe we should talk about this later. You know, when you're able to concentrate better. I mean after all, you need a little time to bask in the moment."

"In the moment?" she says.

Mark replies, "Yeah, in the moment of you getting the chance to make sweet love to me."

Debbie looks at Mark incredulously. "See, you always do that—whenever I want to talk about something serious, you turn it into something silly."

Mark frowns at her and Debbie gives him a cold look.

Mark sighs. "Okay, okay. Yes, I want children, too—just not right now."

"Why not?" she asks. Mark takes her hand.

"Well, right now I'm working on a pretty serious case, and I need to give it my full attention." He smiles at her. "So after it is all over, I will take some time off, and we can make love like rabbits and have a dozen kids."

Debbie laughs. "I love you." she says.

"I love you, too."

They start kissing passionately, but then Mark's cell phone rings. He sighs. "You know, you could ignore it," Debbie says.

"I'd love to, but this could be important information about the case. I've got to take this. Sorry, babe."

Debbie looks at him, disappointed. Mark picks up his cell phone. "Hello?"

Jerome is on the other end of the line. "Hey, Mark. I hope I'm not disturbing you, am I?"

Mark looks over at Debbie and smiles. "Dude, you have really bad timing."

Jerome laughs and apologizes for the interruption. He goes on to say that he's got some information about Sonya.

Mark gets out of bed, excited. "Are you serious? What is it?"

"According to my sources, she's in town, and she's okay. It appears as if he hasn't done anything bad to her," Jerome replies.

"Thank God. I just hope that when this all goes down, we can get her away from him somehow," Mark says.

"Me too. I know how much you want that," Jerome replies.

"Thanks. Talk to you later," Mark says.

"Okay, I'll keep you up to date. Later, man," Jerome replies.

Mark puts his cell phone on the nightstand next to the bed and lies back down, smiling. Debbie says, "I take it all is well with Sonya?"

"Yes. So, hopefully, when this is all done, she can come here and live with us."

Debbie stares at him, her jaw loose. Mark frowns at her. "What?" he asks.

"Does she really have to live here? I mean, you don't really know her," Debbie replies.

"But she's going to need a safe place to stay."

"Mark, I know that you always try to save everybody, but are you sure that it would be wise to let her stay here? I mean, what if you haven't taken down this Mickey guy, wouldn't you be putting our lives in danger by bringing her here? You couldn't really protect her here."

"You're right. I mean, I wasn't even thinking clearly. I just wanted to save her," he says. "How about that old cabin we have? She could stay there. What do you think?"

Debbie nods. "Sounds good, and then maybe your nightmares will stop."

"Yes, it will be good to sleep through the night," he says. Mark tells Debbie that he loves her. Debbie responds, "I love you too, honey." They kiss, and then they get out of bed and go downstairs to eat dinner.

<u>Plotting</u>

Early the next morning, Mickey is in the conference room with his men. "Okay, guys, I have thought about this a lot, and here is how it's going to go down. The best time to hit the bank is first thing in the morning, when it opens at 9:00. Any questions?"

Bullseye responds, "Yeah, I have one. What about the shipment—what time will it arrive?"

Mickey looks annoyed that Bullseye has asked a question, but then he seems to relax, as the question is a good one.

"It will arrive at 8:30 at the train station. Please make sure our guys are on time to pick it up. Any other questions?" Crazy, Money, Informer, Cleaner (Crazy's older brother), Killer, Bone Breaker, Kiss-Up, Bullseye, and Sonya all shake their heads no. Mickey looks pleased.

The Plan

In the police conference room that same morning, Jeff is going over all of the last-minute details. Jeff is pointing at the board and circling things, dividing them into groups.

"All right, guys, listen up. Here is the plan. From the information that was given to us by our inside guys, we know they will probably hit first thing in the morning," says Jeff.

"Wait a minute—what if they decide to rob a lot sooner?" Tim asks.

"Don't worry. Our people on the inside will let us know," Jeff answers. He looks around at everyone. They are all whispering and talking among themselves. "All right, everyone, I need you to be in tip-top shape for Friday. So don't go out and do anything stupid. Our inside guys are keeping an eye on things. I need to see the following people: Mark, Jake, Jerome, and Tim. The rest of you guys are dismissed."

Tim, Jerome, Jake, and Mark wait until everyone leaves.

"Okay, guys, with all the information that was given, we have another situation on our hands here," says Jeff.

"What is it?" Tim asks.

"Well, according to Jake's and Jerome's sources, they're planning on receiving a shipment of cocaine on Friday morning at 8:30— basically, thirty minutes before the bank is hit. We need to have two teams ready to counteract this. I also got word through the grapevine that we might have a spy in our midst. Jake and Jerome, I need you to check this out."

Jake answers, "Yes, sir, we will."

"Tim and Mark, please keep your ears open in case you hear something around the station."

"We will," Mark says. "Do you suspect anyone in particular?"

"No. That's why I need you guys to keep this information between us, okay?"

Mark, Jake, Jerome, and Tim all nod in agreement and leave Jeff's office.

* * *

Back at Mickey's office building, Sonya is walking down the hallway to go and meet with her team. Crazy grabs her arm and pushes her against the wall. Crazy is breathing very heavily on Sonya as he tells her, "Hmmm, I've missed you."

"I don't see how you could, considering we broke up," she replies.

"Oh? When did that happen?"

"You know darn well when that happened," she responds.

Crazy gives a little evil, sexy kind of laugh. "Oh, yes, that's right… last month. Well, I'm so sorry about that. I had some business to do that might have put you in danger, and I couldn't take that risk."

Sonya is unimpressed. "Wow! Crazy, your lies get more elaborate every time I talk to you." Crazy's demeanor changes, and he becomes serious.

"I'm not joking, Sonya. I really was checking on something that could have put your life in danger. Don't worry, though; you will know what it was soon enough," he says.

Sonya's eyes soften a bit. "Well, fine then, but I have to go. My men and I have to go over the plans on how we can get this small group of robbers to pull off this job without getting caught in the first three minutes." She moves to continue down the hall, but Crazy grabs her arm and pulls her back.

"Wait," he says. "Before you go, just one little kiss."

Sonya looks around and says, "All right, just one." Crazy pulls Sonya in close and they kiss. He tells Sonya it's nice and that he'd like another, but Sonya says she can't; she's got to go. Crazy acts like he has given up, but as Sonya starts to leave he pulls her back and pushes her up against the wall, breathing heavily against her again.

"Call me by my real name," he says.

Sonya looks at him and speaks to him in a sexy voice. "James," she says. They begin kissing again, moving from the hallway to an empty office.

Crazy and Sonya are still kissing as they enter the room and begin to rip each other's clothes off. They proceed to have sex in the office on the floor. Twenty minutes later, Sonya shows up at her meeting with her clothing looking out of place. Her team members look at her and then at each other, as if to say, *Okay*.

Sonya sits down and tells her men, "I know that this is just supposed to be a diversion, but I don't see why we can't make a little profit out of this." She looks around at her team with a "we can do this" look on her face.

The men don't want to go against Mickey's wishes, but they know he won't be that upset if they pull this off; besides, it would elevate their status. The men are just about to answer Sonya when Mickey enters the room.

"No!" he says. "I don't want you guys anywhere near that hot zone. We're sending in the worst group, the Scuttlebutts. We don't need any money; we just need them to be captured. You guys just need to keep an eye on them from a distance."

Sonya looks upset, but she knows there is no point in trying to argue with him, because in the end he will win. She merely replies, "Fine. We will stand by."

Mickey has an evil look on his face while he is talking to them. "All right, see you after the plans are complete."

He gives Sonya a dirty look and leaves. She waits until Mickey leaves before speaking to her men. "You heard him—no helping. But I do know one thing: if we were to walk out of this with a big profit, he would get over it. So let's do what we can to help out this group."

Money, who is sitting in on this meeting, says, "But what about what Mickey said? Also, I don't like that look he had on his face."

"Yeah, I know," Sonya says. "You guys get a blueprint of the bank over to the Scuttlebutts."

"I'll take care of everything," Money says. She pulls him aside and thanks him for going along with her. He assures her he has her back no matter what. Money leaves, and Sonya continues to talk to her men.

* * *

That evening, Mark and Debbie are in bed together cuddling.

"So," Debbie says, "are you ready for tomorrow, honey?"

"Yeah. I'm feeling a little nervous, but I know we are going to pull this off tomorrow."

Debbie kisses him. "I know if anyone can pull this off, you can."

Mark holds her closer. "Thanks, honey, I needed to hear that."

The Rundown

Friday morning at 3:00, the alarm clock rings. Mark gets up and goes into the bathroom. He feels nervous and excited at the same time, knowing today is the day he gets Sonya back.

After Mark showers, gets dressed, and brushes his teeth, he heads downstairs to the kitchen. Debbie hands him a cup of coffee. "Good luck, honey," she says.

"Thanks, honey. I can't wait to see you tonight when this is all over with." They kiss and Mark leaves.

At the police station, a lot of officers have arrived. All the cops that are going to be involved in the take down today head to the conference room for a meeting. Jeff is standing up front.

"All right, you guys, you all know the plan. We need to stay on our toes to make sure this goes off without a hitch."

All the cops respond, "Yes, sir."

Jeff tells everyone to be careful and then dismisses them; they all go and get ready to leave.

At the same time, the Scuttlebutts gang is meeting in a small, abandoned warehouse. Jack is talking with his gang that looks like a bunch of rejects who were let in out of pity.

"All right, gang, this is it—our chance to prove to Mickey that we're not losers. If we do this right, maybe we can make him stop calling us Scuttlebutts. Now, let's head out," their leader, Jack, says.

His men cheer, and they get up to leave.

At Mickey's office building, Sonya is talking to her men as they are getting armed. "Okay, men let's go," she says.

They leave, and Bullseye and Kiss-Up and their men all leave, too.

Crazy leaves with his armed men. Killer is walking side-by-side with Crazy when he says, "Crazy, I don't understand why Mickey didn't tell everyone about the truck shipment."

"Because he suspects we have a rat, and he would like to lure it out with some cheese."

"I see," Killer replies.

Everybody is finally situated—the police, and the bad guys.

Bullseye is at the train station, Crazy is at the skyscraper, Sonya is in an apartment across from the bank, and Kiss-Up is at the truck rendezvous point. At 8:30 in the morning, the train arrives right on schedule; the workers at the train station unload the shipment and put it in a warehouse for pickup from different companies. Bullseye and his men are waiting for the workers at the train station to finish storing everything and then leave so that they can go in and get the shipment without trouble.

Meanwhile, at exactly 9:00, the Scuttlebutts run inside the bank to rob it. Back at the train station warehouse, Bullseye and his men take the shipment from the warehouse and load it onto trucks. At the same time, Kiss-Up and his men watch to see what truck their shipment is being switched to, so they can make sure that the truck ends up at the rendezvous point, where the rest of Kiss-Up's guys are waiting. Back at the bank, the Scuttlebutts are standing inside the bank with their guns drawn. Everyone inside is frozen with fear.

"All right, this is a stick up. Everyone down on the ground," Jack yells. He points his gun at the teller, hands her a bag, and instructs her to fill it. The teller nods and begins filling up the bag with money.

After she is done, they lock all the bank tellers in one vault, and all of the customers in another vault. The Scuttlebutts begin to make their escape through the bank's back door. Once outside, the

Scuttlebutts are caught by the police, who are waiting with weapons drawn.

"All right, scumbags, hands up!" Jerome yells.

Jack replies in a nervous voice, "That's Scuttlebutts, not Scumbags."

"What?" Jerome asks.

"Our name is Scuttlebutts; you said our name was Scumbags."

Jerome walks up to Jack. "Excuse me. Your name is whatever I say it is, you got that? And by the way, this goes for all of you: you shouldn't be talking anyway, unless you want to incriminate yourself and save us the time of sending you to trial, where you will be sent to prison to become some inmate's girl."

Jerome looks at the Scuttlebutts' leader and one of the men standing next to him, and says, "I can tell that you're going to be pretty popular when you guys go in."

After Jerome's rousing statement, Jack pees himself. The cops are shocked to see such a display of fear. Tim walks over to Jerome and pats him on the shoulder. "Oh, man. I'm just glad that you didn't scare the you-know-what out of them, Jerome."

Ben one of the officers with Tim and Jerome looks at one of the men that was next to Jack and is grossed out. "Too late; looks like this guy went above and beyond the call of duty."

Everyone looks back at that guy and sees brown stains of a bowel movement on his pants. The cops are grossed out and start putting the Scuttlebutts into the paddy wagon. While all this is happening, Sonya and her men are watching everything from a safe distance in an empty apartment close by.

"Looks like everything went off without a hitch," she says. "I just think it's a little strange, though, that the police were there so quickly." She stares out the window, confused. The men in the room gather up their stuff to leave.

"I guess we can go report back to my father," Sonya says.

As she and her men are about to leave, a group of masked and armed men bursts through the door and start shooting at them. Sonya is knocked to the ground by one of her men who is trying to keep her from getting killed, but not before she gets hit in her side by one of the bullets. The police bust in right behind the gunmen and take them down. Then they start checking Sonya and her men, as well as the masked gunmen, for survivors.

Tim walks over to Sonya, kneels down beside her, and checks her out all over. He looks around for Ben and tells him to come over. Sonya is watching Tim and Ben while clutching her side. Tim notices the wound and how much blood Sonya has lost.

"I see it," Tim says to Sonya, and touches her on her head gently.

He turns to Ben and instructs him to make sure an ambulance is on the way. Ben nods and walks off. Jerome walks up to Tim and asks for a status report. Tim tells Jerome, "She is alive, but barely."

Tim turns his attention back to Sonya, and puts his hand on the wound to help stop the bleeding. "Just hang in there; help is on the way."

Jerome comes over and looks at Sonya. She looks up at Jerome and then passes out. Tim checks her to make sure she is all right.

"Is this her?" Jerome asks. When Tim nods, Jerome adds, "Well, Miss Sonya, please live; your big brother Mark will be very happy to see you."

A cop walks over to Jerome and whispers something to him while Tim strokes Sonya's face gently.

"We have two more who are still alive, but I don't think they'll make it," Jerome tells Tim.

"Who are these men?" Tim asks.

Jerome takes off one of the shooters' masks. He looks at the shooter and is shocked. "These are Assassin's men, and you know as well as I do that Assassin works for Mickey."

Tim stares at Assassin's guy. "What? Is—"

"Yes," Jerome interrupts."These men work for Mickey. It looks like Mickey sent Assassin's men here to kill her. I wonder why?"

"Beats me," Tim responds. "That man has always been nuts."

He looks at Sonya and shakes his head. "Jeff and his team should be moving in to capture Mickey, and we can ask Mickey when we see him."

Over at the train station warehouse, Bullseye and his men are gathering the last of the shipment when Mark and the other cops come busting in with their guns drawn. "Hands up!" Mark shouts.

Bullseye and his crew look surprised as they all get taken into custody. Mark turns and looks at his fellow officer Sheila and says, "Well, that takes care of this group. I hope the other guys are having good luck."

Sheila responds, "Me too."

At the same time, Jake and his squad watch Kiss-Up and his crew arrive at the rendezvous point off Highway 10 on a deserted road. Kiss-Up sees the truck arrive, and then his men unload the drugs from the truck. Jake and his squad move in to capture Kiss-Up and his crew.

"All right, guys, hands up!" Jake shouts.

Kiss-Up and his men look completely surprised and a bit disappointed. Kiss-Up shakes his head and says to his men, "Oh great! We've been set up."

"You sure were!" Jake replies."Now, shut up, fool, and listen to me as I read you your rights."

On a nearby hilltop, while all of these different events are happening, Crazy, Killer, and Bone Breaker are all watching everything that is happening to Kiss-Up and his group. "Good," says Crazy. "It looks like it went off the way it was supposed to at the truck delivery. How did things go off at the train station?"

Killer responds, "Just as you thought—the cops were there waiting for them."

"Good, good," Crazy replies."Now, is Sonya safe?"

"Informer has not reported back to me yet."

"All right," Crazy says. "Let me know as soon as Informer reports in."

Bone Breaker and Killer both nod.

Over at Mickey's hideout, Jeff and his men storm in, capturing Mickey and his remaining men. Two officers walk Mickey over to Jeff.

"Well, well, well, looks like we've caught ourselves a big fish here. Mickey, what happened to you? Seems like you're losing your touch," Jeff says.

Mickey has an evil smirk on his face as he responds, "Maybe."

"I guess if you weren't so busy trying to kill your daughter, maybe you wouldn't have been here to get captured," Jeff says.

Mickey looks at Jeff with a psychotic look, and laughs. "Don't you try to school me on what I'm supposed to do. She isn't my real daughter. She's just a stand-in to be disposed of whenever it pleases me."

"You're sick," Jeff says. "Get him out of my sight."

Two officers haul Mickey off. He turns around while they're taking him away and says, "What's wrong, Jeff? Did you want me to answer you differently?"

He starts laughing sinisterly as they continue to haul him away. Informer is watching everything from a safe distance on top of a skyscraper that has a view of everything, except where Kiss-Up had been. He calls Crazy and tells him how everything is going off, just like they planned. He also tells Crazy about the whole situation with Sonya.

"Well, it looks like you were right," Informer says. "Mickey did have something bad planned for her. The police came in just in the nick of time."

"Where is she now?" Crazy asks.

"She is being taken to the hospital. Looks like she's wounded badly, but I think she will survive. I'll get the information from the hospital about her status. As soon as I do and we know she is better, we can retrieve her," Informer replies.

"I had a feeling he would try something, and you're right about leaving her there at the hospital. I want her healed before we move her. Besides, she's safer there until we complete my plan."

"Yes, boss," Informer says.

Crazy also tells Informer to keep up with Mickey. "I don't want anything to go wrong, because if it does and Mickey finds out, we are all dead, do you understand?"

Informer tells Crazy he understands then ends the call.

The Aftermath

Mark gets a call on his cell phone from Jerome, who informs him about what happened at the apartment.

"I'm glad to hear she's okay," Mark says. "I'll swing by and see her before I go home."

"All right. See you later, "Jerome replies.

At the police station, Jeff is sitting at his desk when Tim walks into his office. "Yes, Tim, what is it?"

"Mickey's lawyer is here, sir."

"Send him in."

Jeff brother Eric walks into Jeff's office. "Well, Jeff, looks like you are still playing the good guy," he says.

"Eric! How nice to see you. What are you doing here?"

Eric smirks and tells Jeff, "I'm here for my client. I hope you're not questioning him without his lawyer."

"Eric, why do you defend people like him?" Jeff says. "You know he's bad; why do you do it?"

"Because the money is good, and the women are fine. Listen, little brother, don't question me about my reasons, okay?"

"I'm not," says Jeff. "I'm just trying to figure lawyers like you out."

"Oh, I see. Well, that will just remain a mystery, won't it?"

Jeff replies, "Yes, big brother, I guess it will; I can't understand you."

"Don't try to, okay? Mom and Dad didn't understand me either when they were around."

"That's not true, Eric. They cared about you, as I do," says Jeff. "What happened to you?"

"I grew up, and I stopped playing around," Eric says. "Don't worry about me, Jeff. I'll be fine." Jeff starts to reply, but Eric interrupts him. "I've got to go, little bro. Take care."

He gets up, and when he gets to the door, he turns around and looks at Jeff. "Oh, and by the way, my client will be out of here within the hour."

Jeff stands up. "That's not possible!"

Eric laughs. "Just watch me," he says, and leaves Jeff's office.

Tim comes in right after. "Sir, are you okay?"

Jeff shakes his head. "Yeah, I just got some family issues."

"Oh. I understand, sir. Sometimes family can be your worst enemy."

Jeff looks at Tim curiously. Tim never talks about his family situation or his past. "Do you have any brothers?" Jeff asks.

"What?" Tim asks like he doesn't understand the question. "Anyway, sir, whatever his reasons are, we don't know. The only way to help him is to get the people over Eric, starting with Mickey. So we need to make sure that the drug charges stick."

Jeff smiles. "You're right; it may be the only way we can help Sonya for Mark, too." he says. Tim agrees, and only then does Jeff realize Tim had avoided answering the question about siblings. *He must really like to keep his private life private. I'm going to try and get him to tell me something.*

Jeff is about to ask Tim a question when Jerome pokes his head into the office. "Look who I have here," he says with excitement. Jeff and Tim both look at Jerome with curious expressions, wondering who it is. Their question is answered when Bullseye pops into Jeff's office.

Tim and Jeff smile and laugh as they walk up to him. "Ah, man, great to see you again. It's been too long since you left to go undercover. Things sure have been boring around here without you," Tim says. He shakes Bullseye's hand and gives him a pat on the back.

"Yeah, man, it's great to see you back home safe." He shakes Bullseye's hand and gives him an approving nod.

"It has definitely been too long, "Bullseye replies.

"Aren't you worried that when they find out what you've done, they'll kill you?" Tim asks.

"Well, I'm a little worried, but I think I have an ace up my sleeve," Bullseye says with a concerned look.

"And what exactly would that be?" Jeff asks.

Bullseye smiles. "Well, sir, I'm the one who told the cops about where Sonya and her men were. So basically, you could say I saved her life."

"I see," Jeff says. "And you think Mickey will keep you alive because of that?"

Bullseye shakes his head. "No, I think Crazy will. I think that guy is more powerful than we think he is. By the way, how is she?"

Jeff tells him that Sonya was wounded badly, but she is going to be okay.

"The bullet didn't do any real damage to her organs. So this will help her pull through a lot better," Jeff says.

Bullseye seems pleased and tells everyone that he will talk with them later.

"Where are you going?" Tim asks.

"Home. I've missed the old place."

"Do you think that's wise?" Jeff asks, looking puzzled.

"Yes, I do. Besides, they don't know where I live, and I have my insurance policy—Sonya."

Jeff looks concerned. "I'm against this, but all right. However, if you think anything is strange, I want you to come back here immediately. Call me anytime, Bullseye."

"Yes, sir," Bullseye replies. "Goodbye, guys. Tell Mark hi for me."

Bullseye leaves and Jerome shakes his head. "I hope for his sake he doesn't do anything stupid." He gives Tim a look as if to say, "You know what I mean."

Jerome leaves to go check on Mark at the hospital, and Tim is heading out the door as well when Jeff stops him.

"What did Jerome mean by that?" he asks.

Tim sighs and answers, "Well, it's just that Mark's wife, Debbie, use to go out with Bullseye, and then she dumped him for Mark."

Jeff is shocked at the news. "Really? I thought that was Jake."

"No, Jake was before Bullseye."

Jeff looks more confused than ever. Tim can see that Jeff doesn't understand what is going on, so he tries to tell him what he knows.

"Bullseye told Jerome and me that he never stopped sleeping with Debbie when her and Mark started dating, and that he asked her to choose between him and Mark. She chose Mark, of course. After that, she went to Mark and confessed everything. They worked out all of their problems, and then they got married."

"Wait," Jeff says.

"What is it, sir?" Tim asks.

"How long have Mark and Debbie been married?"

"Two years," Tim replies.

"When exactly did Bullseye leave for his two-year undercover operation?"

Tim nods. "I see what you're getting at, sir, and so did Jerome. He tried to warn Mark, but Mark wanted to give her a chance to prove that she wasn't still messing around with Bullseye. And whatever happened on the night of Mark's wedding between Debbie and Bullseye must have been big. He left the night after the wedding to go work undercover as one of Mickey's men."

Jeff can't believe what he is hearing. "How was Mark when this all went down?"

"Mark says that he has forgiven them, but he still doesn't trust Bullseye. I can't say I blame him."

Jeff looks upset. "What the heck is going on around here? Am I running a soap opera, or what?"

Tim assures Jeff that he is not. He starts to leave, but before he goes out the door, he turns around. "Sir, I would suggest you talk to Jerome; he can be quite informative," he says.

"Thanks. I'll do that."

"I just hope Bullseye has gotten over her during these past two years," Tim adds, and then leaves Jeff's office.

***

Mark arrives at the Metro Hospital and heads inside Sonya's hospital room. She is patched up and awake in bed.

"Hi. I'm Mark," he says.

"Hi," Sonya replies.

"Sonya, I wanted to ask you a question. Do you feel up to it?" She shrugs. "Sure."

"Do I look familiar to you?" Mark asks.

She studies Mark and then replies, "Not really. Should I know you?"

"Well, it's been many years since you and I have seen each other. You were a little girl about five years old the last time you saw me, and I looked differently then."

Sonya is trying to search her memory, but she can't place Mark. But, going over what she remembers, she tells Mark she doesn't remember everybody's face. She asks if he was one of the gangster kids that her parents would let her hang out with. Mark nods.

"Yes. I was the boy that would always make sure you had something to eat and some place to sleep."

"I do remember a little of that, but ever since the day my mom took me to Mickey I can't really remember anything," Sonya says.

"It's understandable. Why don't I fill in the blanks?" Mark says.

Sonya tells Mark that would be great. He starts telling Sonya what it was like living in the abandoned warehouse. He also tells her what happened that day after her mother took her away. Mark tells her about his personal life in hopes to get her to talk about hers. He and Sonya are becoming acquainted with each other, and Mark is glad that Sonya seems to be a good person.

"So, Mark, tell me about this wife of yours."

"She's great, and she has a kind heart. I know that once the two of you get to know each other you'll be very good friends."

"I'm sure we will, or at least we'll be polite to each other," she replies. "So, was it love at first sight?"

Mark looks down, a bit embarrassed, and then looks at Sonya. She wonders why he's giving that look, but she can tell he is not ready to talk about it. So she just lets him tell her whatever he wants for the time being.

Sonya asks, "How has it been for you two?"

"Fine. There were two other men fighting for her at the time, but I was the man that won her heart."

"Oh? Tell me about it."

Mark tells Sonya about Jake first, and then he talks about Bullseye. When Mark mentions Bullseye, Sonya is shocked to find out that he is a cop. She wonders to herself, *Could Bullseye be the one Mickey has been looking for?* Mark interrupts her thoughts.

"I never stopped trying to get to you. I was finally able to find out where you were, thanks to Jerome. I just didn't know how to get to you safely," he says.

Mark and Sonya smile at each other and hold hands. Mark asks Sonya what was it like for her with Mickey, why she stayed with him, and what she has been up to in her personal life besides the criminal activities. She takes a deep breath and begins to tell Mark about what it has been like for her.

"I guess I should tell you what happened when I arrived at Mickey's house after my mother was killed." Mark encourages her to continue. "He introduced me to his wife first. She seemed very cold. Then he introduced me to his children. They seemed to look down on me. He had Gossip show me to my room."

"Did they mistreat you?" he asks.

"Not physically, but they acted like I didn't exist. I was all alone, until I met some friends…"

Sonya is interrupted by Jerome's arrival. "All right, what is going on here?" Jerome asks as he walks into Sonya's hospital room.

Mark turns around and replies, "Oh, hi, Jerome. What are you doing here?"

"Making sure you stay focused." He gives Mark a disapproving look.

"I assure you, I am," he replies.

"Mark, we don't have time for a walk down memory lane. I'll take over the questioning from now on."

Mark tries to stop him, but Jerome pushes past him and walks up to Sonya. "Look, we don't have a lot of time to waste, so I'm going to play bad cop here, if I have to," he says.

"Jerome—"

Sonya interrupts. "It's all right, Mark. I'll answer him."

Jerome responds, "Good, I'm glad we're on the same page. Let's get started. I want to know everything that happened at the bank robbery today. Also, who was the real boss over today's activities? I know it's not you, because you wouldn't have gotten yourself shot. Is there any plan for more drug shipments?"

Sonya looks over at Mark for approval. He gives Sonya a nod to go ahead.

"Mickey planned the whole thing," she says."And he always keeps a copy of his plans on his computer."

Jerome and Mark are shocked. "Are you serious?" Jerome asks.

Sonya says, "Yes. Now, of course, it's not visible to the naked eye. It might be encrypted. If you don't see it there, check his wife's computer."

"What type of stuff do you think is on his computer that would allow us to prosecute him?" Jerome asks. Sonya thinks for a moment as the two officers watch her.

"I thought of something. I hope this will be enough. He uses an alias when he is expecting a shipment, so if you can tie the alias to him, then you've got him," she says.

Mark and Jerome exchange glances. "Does he use this alias outside of his criminal activities?" Mark asks.

"Yes. Whenever he takes trips and gets speeding tickets, he uses his alias. So you should have them in your records. Also, another thing is that when he arranges the shipment, he signs the paperwork." She stops and looks at Jerome and Mark, confused.

"What?" Mark asks.

Sonya replies, "I can't believe you guys had someone on the inside, and you did not know this already. Hasn't that guy been telling you anything?"

Mark and Jerome look at each other and nod in agreement.

"That is a good question. Jerome, you need to check your informers and tell Jake to check his," Mark says.

"I will," Jerome replies. "I'll have the guys check for his alias signature, and match it against his real signature to prove that he was the one who masterminded all of these plans over the years."

Mark smiles. "We've got him."

Sonya lies back in bed. Mark turns to her with concern. "What's wrong?"

"Nothing, I'm just really tired now," she says. Mark takes her hand.

"Well then, rest, and I will come and see you later," he tells her.

"All right, Mark. I look forward to seeing you again, and I'm glad I could help."

Mark watches Sonya close her eyes, and then he and Jerome leave the hospital room.

"Well, what do you want to do now?" Jerome asks.

"We've got a lot of things, including getting a warrant to look at Mickey's wife's computer," he answers.

"The DA will work on that. Why don't you go home to your wife, and get some rest. Maybe you can dig around some more into getting evidence against Mickey to save Sonya from him. From what I'm hearing, his lawyer will get him off soon."

"Okay, while you guys get that sorted, I'll take a break at home and hang out with my wife a bit. First thing in the morning, I'll look everything over," Mark replies.

"Sounds like a plan, see you later," Jerome says. Mark says goodbye to Jerome and then leaves to go home.

A Tragedy

Once Mark arrives home he goes inside, grabs Debbie, and kisses her. "It's just you and me tonight," he says.

Debbie smiles and tells him she's going to fix him a good dinner tonight of steak and potatoes, and for dessert, home baked cherry pie. Mark tells her that sounds great; he'll go take a shower while she is cooking.

Mark heads upstairs to the bathroom when the phone rings. Debbie answers the phone. "Hello," she says. She tells the caller to hold on and goes and gets Mark.

"Mark, it's the record clerk, Gina, on the phone."

Mark picks up the phone "Hello?"

"How's Cleo doing?" Gina asks using the code that Mark told her to use.

"Great. So what have you been up to?" Mark asks.

"Oh nothing, just that it's a doggie dog world you know."

"True," replies Mark.

"You know, my friend got $730."

Mark remembers their earlier conversion in Gina's office when he told her how they should contact each other in code. He looks at the clock to see what time it is. Six forty-five pm. "You don't say."

Mark tells Gina he's got to go—his wife is calling him—and that he will talk to her later. They say their goodbyes and then Mark goes and tells Debbie that he's got some police business and that he will be back later.

"Sure," she says in a sarcastic tone.

Mark caresses Debbie's face. "We will talk about this when I get home."

He kisses Debbie goodbye and then leaves to go to the theatre to meet Gina. Mark arrives at the movie theatre and checks around to make sure he hasn't been followed. Then, he goes inside.

He buys a ticket for the movie, *I Love My Dog*, playing at 7:30 pm. He walks inside the theatre and sees Gina sitting in the back row, up against the left side wall. She turns and spots him. He walks over to her. While he is doing this he is also taking observation of who is around in the theatre. No one seems out of place.

Mark sits down next to Gina. "So what is it?" he asks.

"Well…"

He interrupts Gina. "Wait a minute, were you followed?"

"No, no," she replies.

"Okay, sorry. Continue."

"Well, like I was about to say, I started to hang out with my friend from the IA records room, and he told me that one of the guys has been looking at the files for the policemen at our precinct."

"Oh really?" Mark replies, surprised. "Why would he be doing this? As far as I know no one at our office has done anything to warrant an investigation."

"That's what I was thinking," she says. "I tried to get him to give me more information about it but he wouldn't."

"Oh man, we have got to find out who the agent is, and get a hold of that information," Mark replies.

"Yes, that's also what I was thinking. So I did some digging and—" But just as Gina was about to finish her statement, a group of people sat in front of her and Mark. "Anyways…" Gina whispers as one of the people in front of them turns around and says, "Shh."

Gina is about to continue when Mark notices one of the people in the group is eavesdropping on the conversation.

Mark motions for Gina to follow him. They leave the theatre. Mark does a quick look around, and all looks clear. They walk down the sidewalk to finish the conversation. "So, do you know who it is?" Mark asks.

"Yes. I finally got my friend to get me some more information. He told me that the guy was checking into *you*," Gina says.

"Me?" Mark replies, shocked. "Why? I've done nothing wrong."

"I know, but apparently during your investigation into trying to get Sonya back you must have stumbled onto something."

"I don't know what," Mark says.

"I looked over everything we found in those files, and the answer was closer then we thought. Mark, both our lives are in serious danger from what I discovered," Gina says.

"Don't worry, Gina, I can protect you."

She gives a sigh of relief. "Okay. You are not going to believe this, but it's that agent guy—"

Before Gina can finish her statement, a gun shot sounds. A bullet hits Gina in the head, and then hits the concrete wall of the building next to her. Gina falls down, dead.

Mark kneels down next to her body in shock, and double checks her vitals. She is dead. People that were walking around saw what happened begin to panic, running and screaming as they try to get out of there. Mark yells out to everyone to stay calm, but nobody is listening. He stays crouched down and looks around, but sees no one with a gun. He gets on his cell phone and calls for backup. Jerome and Sheila arrive on the scene soon after to see other officers taping off the area where Gina got shot. They are making sure everybody stays back and are questioning possible witnesses.

Jerome goes to one of the officers collecting evidence.

"Do you know what happened here?" he asks.

"Yeah," the officer replies. "The records clerk, Gina, was walking with Mark on the sidewalk over there when she got shot in the head. The bullet is in the wall over there."

Jerome asks the officer where Mark is. The officer points to the coffee house across the street. Jerome goes over to Sheila and informs her what is going on they go inside the coffee house. Inside, it's an average looking coffee house with tables and chairs, a couch, and places for Wi-Fi.

Jerome and Sheila see Mark sitting in a booth. He looks shaken up.

"Hey how's it going?" Jerome asks.

Mark looks up at Jerome and Sheila and then down, shamefully. Sheila squats next to Mark and puts her hand on his. "Do you want us to call Debbie?"

Mark nods. "Okay."

Sheila stands up and says to Jerome, "I'll call his wife while you keep him company."

Jerome pulls a chair in front of Mark and sits down. "Hey, come on, man talk to me."

Mark looks up at Jerome. "I told her I would protect her."

"Hey, don't do that, man. We've all been in that position."

"Yeah, but...I endangered her life, and now she's dead. It's all my fault. I just had to get her involved," Mark says.

"Come on, it's not your fault, okay?" Jerome replies.

"You don't understand," Mark says.

"So help me understand. What is going on?" Jerome asks.

He doesn't answer right away. He thinks that if he tells Jerome and Sheila what he knows, he might be putting them in danger, too. "I don't know myself. She said she had something to say, and then she got shot before she could say it."

"I see," says a man's voice. It sounds familiar to Mark. *Where have I heard that voice before?* He looks at the doorway to the coffee shop that was across the street from the movie theatre, and sees the IA agent, Todd, coming inside.

When Mark sees him, he realizes he made the right move in staying quiet.

"Who are you?" Mark asks, pretending not to know.

"Smith from Internal Affairs," he replies. "So, she didn't say anything?"

"No. I wish she had. Maybe then her death wouldn't have been in vain," Mark replies.

"Hmmm. Well, it looks like my work here is done," Todd says.

"What do you mean?" Mark asks.

"I just came here to make sure it wasn't friendly fire," Todd replies. "You know how that is. You look tired. You should get some rest," he adds in a snarky tone.

Mark wants to get up and strangle Todd, but he recalls what Gina told him about an agent at Internal Affairs investigating him. He begins to wonder if it's this Todd guy. He finds it strange that he go there so fast, or that he is here at all. *I've got to get a hold of Gina's friend in the IA records department.*

"Mark," Sheila says, interrupting his thoughts. "Your wife says she can't come. She says she's been drinking and that she is going to go to sleep. So, I'll take you home, if that's okay?"

"Sure. What about my car?" Mark asks.

"I'll have the guys take it to the station and look over it to make sure the perpetrator didn't leave any prints or anything. You can pick it up in the morning. I'll give you a ride to work," Jerome says.

Sheila turns to Todd. "I'm going to take him home now, if that's all right?"

"Yeah, yeah, that's fine. I'm leaving, too; I've got no reason to stay," Todd says, then leaves to go home.

"Come on, Mark, let's go. Jerome, I'll talk to you later," Sheila says.

Jerome nods and Mark leaves with Sheila. As she drops Mark off at home, they both notice that Debbie's car is in the driveway, and not in the garage.

"I'll walk you up to the door," Sheila says.

"No need, I have a feeling I'll be safe," Mark replies.

"Are you sure?"

"Yes. I'll be fine."

"Okay, but if you need anything, Jerome, Tim, and I will be there for you whenever or whatever you need," she says.

Mark smiles. "I know." He gets out of the car and waves goodbye. Mark is walking up to the front door and wondering just how much drinking Debbie has done so that she couldn't come and get him, and why her car is in the driveway and not in the garage, where it was when he'd left.

Once Mark is inside the house, he takes off his shoes, hangs up his jacket, and goes upstairs. He pauses when he gets upstairs; he can hear the TV going.

"What the..." he says to himself. Mark opens the door to the bedroom, and there is Debbie sitting in bed watching TV and texting. She sees Mark in the doorway, but chooses not to acknowledge him.

"Okay," Mark says as he enters the room. Debbie turns off the TV and looks at him.

"What?" she asks.

"Oh, nothing. I just needed you, and you weren't there for me, that's all," Mark replies.

"Mark, I've been thinking about things, and I realize I made a mistake a long time ago," Debbie says.

"Where is this coming from? Do you even care about what just happened to me?" Mark asks.

"I do, it's just that I..." She pauses. "Mark you are always trying to save everybody, or do everything. I just don't want to deal with it anymore, okay?"

"So what are you trying to say? Do you want to leave me?" he asks.

"No, not really," she replies.

"What does that mean? No, not really?"

"It means I love you, but I don't want to talk about it right now."

"I think we should," Mark says.

"Well, I don't. Goodnight," she says. Debbie turns off her cell phone and her lamp, and lies down in the bed.

"Fine," Mark says. He goes into the bathroom, and Debbie yells that he can just go sleep on the couch. Mark tells her fine, he will. He wishes he could have driven home; that way he could have gone to a nice hotel room. But he's still glad he let them take the car to check it out. After all, they need to make sure no bombs were put on the car. Mark goes and sleeps on the couch.

He spends most of the night tossing and turning before giving up. He gets up and gets dressed, and decides to call a cab. He'll go over to Gina's place to see if he can find anything. When Mark arrives he can see the cops are still there.

"Have you guys found anything?" he asks.

"Nope. We haven't checked her bedroom yet though," Tim says.

"I'll look in there," Mark says. He goes into the bedroom and looks around but sees nothing that catches his eye.

Then he asks Tim if anyone got Gina's cell phone, and if they did, what was on it.

"Our expert's Dwayne and Samson are looking at it now back at the station," Tim answers as he hands Mark his car keys. "Why don't you take my car over there? I can just get a ride back with one of these guys."

Mark takes the car keys. "Thanks, Tim, I really appreciate it."

"No problem."

Mark thanks Tim again and then leaves to go to the station.

Freedom

Over at the police station, Mickey's personal limo is waiting outside for Mickey. The police station doors open, and Mickey comes out and gets in the limo. Eric is already sitting inside when Mickey gets in. Eric tells the driver that they're ready to go, and the limo leaves the police station.

Mickey gives Eric an evil look. "So, what took you so long?"

"I had to cut through all the red tape to get you out, Mickey," Eric replies.

"Don't give me excuses, Eric. If you can't handle the job, then you can easily be replaced, understand?"

"Yes, sir," Eric replies.

The limo pulls up at Mickey's home, but Mickey looks upset when he sees where they are. "What are we doing here?"

"I thought you would want to go home," Eric says.

Mickey looks at Eric with disgust. "Do I pay you to think for me?"

Eric replies, nervously, "No, sir, I just thought that—"

Mickey slaps him in the face.

"Did I ask you for all that?" Mickey snaps. Eric stares at Mickey, so frightened he can't even speak."Did I?" Mickey yells.

Eric curls up in the fetal position. "No, sir," he responds. Mickey seems pleased with Eric's response.

"Good. Yes or no is all I want to hear from you," he says. He then turns in the driver's direction. "*Driver!*"

"Yes, sir?"

Mickey tells him to take him to his office, and the limo pulls away from Mickey's home.

At the same time inside Jeff's office, Jeff is talking to Sheila. "Okay, tell Mark and the rest of the officers that we've got the warrant, so we can head over to Mickey's home and office to check them out," he says.

"Great," Sheila says. "I've been looking forward to this all day."

Everyone at the police station starts getting ready to leave.

Over at Mickey's office, the limo comes to a stop, and Mickey gets out. He turns to look at Eric, who is still sitting in the limo. "Are you coming?" Mickey asks.

"No, I have to check on what the police are up to. And I have to meet with the district attorney," Eric replies.

"All right. See you later, then," says Mickey. He closes the door, and the limo drives away as Mickey enters the building.

Mickey begins walking down the hallway, talking to himself while looking around. He wonders where everybody is. He arrives at his office and goes inside, where he sees Assassin and his men chained to the walls around his office.

"What is the meaning of this?" Mickey exclaims. Assassin is screaming about how he can't believe that he is here—all he did was follow Mickey's orders and sent his men to kill Sonya. This is the thanks he gets? The office door closes behind Mickey once he fully enters the office.

Mickey turns and tries to open the door, but he can't. He hears something ticking and turns around, but he sees nothing. Then he sees Assassin and his men looking up. Mickey looks up as well and sees a bomb attached to the light fixtures on the ceiling.

"Oh, shoot!" Mickey yells. He tries to get out through the window by stepping up on a chair, but the glass won't break, and the window is sealed shut. Mickey looks at the bomb; it starts to count down. Five, four, three, two, one, zero…then nothing happens. Mickey laughs and starts to relax a bit; suddenly, the phone rings in his office.

He picks up the phone. "Hello?"

Cleaner is on the other end of the line. "Did you enjoy the joke?" he asks.

"What?"

"The joke," Cleaner repeats."Did you enjoy it?"

"Of course not!"

"Oh, sorry about that…then you are not going to enjoy this one either. You better look at the floor under the rug in your secret compartment."

Mickey drops the phone and runs around his desk to the rug. He lifts it up and looks in the compartment in the floor. To his dismay, the compartment has a bomb in it.

Assassin and his men's eyes get big. They struggle even harder to get out of the chains, but to no avail. Assassin pleads, "Mickey, please help us."

"I don't have time for that," Mickey snaps."I'm trying to get out so that *I* can live."

Assassin responds, "After all we've…I've done for you…"

"Well, I thought you were top-notch assassins; can't you get yourselves out of some weak chains?" Mickey laughs. "Don't act so surprised—you knew the risks in working for me. You know that I look out for myself, first and foremost. Stop being such a wimp. Death looks good on you, don't cha think?"

Assassin screams. Mickey continues trying to find a way out while Assassin and his men struggle to escape. The bomb in the floor switches on and starts counting down: five, four, three, two, one, zero…nothing. Everyone breathes a sigh of relief.

"Oh, thank God, another joke. There is no way I'm going to die at the hands of some stupid punks," Mickey says.

Just then, the cabinet next to the window pops open, revealing a sign inside: *Too bad, douche bag. This is not a joke.* Mickey looks around, panicked. He looks out the window, and can see a silhouette of a man with long hair. A tear rolls down Mickey's cheek. "Oh…!" Before Mickey can finish his statement, the explosives in the cabinet detonate.

The room is disintegrated first, and then the whole building goes up in smoke. Bone Breaker and Cleaner are watching the whole thing from a safe distance, on a monitor in Bone Breaker's car. All the cops from Mark's precinct at the station and on patrol hear a call over the radio about an explosion over at Mickey's office. Mark gets on the radio. "We should be there within minutes; we were already on the way."

Jeff and another officer are in the car, driving to the scene. Jeff gets on the radio and responds to Mark. "Good. I want to know what is going on over there."

The police arrive to see the building in ruins. Tim and Jerome arrive in separate unmarked cars. Jerome looks around in disbelief. "What the…"

Tim interrupts him. "My thoughts exactly."

Sheila walks around, taking everything in. "All right, ladies and gentlemen don't just stand there. It's safe now; we can start checking everything. Be sure not to contaminate the scene," she says.

All the police officers on site say, "Yes, ma'am," and move to investigate the scene. Sheila monitors the other cops as they check the place out. Two of the investigators call over to her. "We've found something," one says.

Sheila, Mark, Jerome, Tim, and Jake go over to take a look. Jeff arrives on the scene and joins them. They see a number of charred bodies. One of the bodies has Mickey's ring on, so they believe it's safe to assume that it's him. The other body has a gold tooth, like Assassin. They see the other bodies and come to the conclusion that they are Assassin's men.

"Have you gotten everything that we will need for the investigation?" Sheila asks one of the cops named Rick.

"Yeah, we got just about everything," he replies.

"Good, go ahead and inform the coroner he can take the bodies," Sheila replies. She then adds, "One thing I think everyone wants to know is, why was Assassin and his men all in chains?"

"Those poor souls didn't even have a chance," Tim says.

"Yeah, you're right. I really feel sorry for them," Mark says.

Jake, Jerome, and Tim look at Mark like he's crazy. "I'm kidding! I hate to say this, but I'm glad they're dead," Mark says.

Jerome agrees. "Now we have to find out who killed them," he says.

"Well, at least we know one thing at this point," Mark says. Jake, Tim, and Jerome look at him quizzically.

"We know something has happened to Mickey. Whether he's dead or alive, we know something major just tookplace," Mark explains. They all agree.

"I guess we should still continue with our investigation," Jerome says. "It should lead us to some answers."

"You're right," Mark replies. "We should still investigate so we can make sure his empire is taken down with him."

"I'm glad you agree with me; anything else we should do?" Jerome asks.

"Nope," Mark replies. "We're already going to run several tests just to make sure that Mickey's body is definitely one of them, and that he won't be coming back somehow."

"I couldn't agree with you more," Jeff replies. "Maybe once all the dust has settled, my brother and Sonya can feel free enough to leave."

Mark nods. "I'm sure they will."

"So, do you guys have any ideas on who could have killed these people?" Sheila asks.

"No," Mark replies. "But I know who might."

Sheila frowns at him. "Who?"

"Sonya. I'll go to the hospital and ask if she knows of anyone who would want Mickey dead." Jerome wants to go with Mark, but Jeff says no, they have too much investigating to do.

"I think Mark can handle this on his own," Jeff adds.

"So what do we do?" Jake asks.

Jeff is about to speak when his cell phone rings. He answers his cell and then after two minutes he ends the call.

"Okay, guys, I've got to go," he says. "I've told Tim what I would like for you guys to do, so listen to him for your assignments. If any of you need me, I'll be back at the station."

Tim starts handing out orders. "Okay, guys, this is how we're going to do this. Jake and I will go check out Mickey's house and see what is on that computer."

Jake nods in agreement. Tim then looks at Sheila and Jerome. "You two will go check out the morgue."

"Okay," Sheila says. "What do you want us to do there?"

"I want you to check with Doc to see if he can confirm that it is Mickey's body." Tim turns to Mark. "You already have your assignment."

Mark nods, and Tim tells everyone to make sure they stay in touch. Then they all leave to go do their assignments. That evening, Tim and Jake are the first to get started on their assignment. They arrive at Mickey's house and knock on the door.

Jake and Tim can hear someone inside, but no one is saying anything. "We are police officers, and we need to come inside and speak to the lady of the house," Jake says.

Jolene, Mickey's forty-two-year-old, blonde wife, cracks the door. "Not without a search warrant," she says.

Tim replies, "Then it's a good thing we got one. Now, let us in."

Jolene lets them in. After they step inside, Jake says, "All right, guys, I want this place checked from top to bottom."

Tim heads over to Jolene, who is pacing around frantically.

"You guys have no right to touch anything in our house; you have no proof of anything," she says.

"Well, actually we do. It's called a search warrant. You should have tried paying attention when we were telling you that earlier at the door."

"Wait until my husband gets home—he'll kill you," she says.

"I'm afraid your husband won't be killing anybody," he replies. "He's is no longer with us. Sorry to tell you."

"What?" she cries.

"Your husband is dead," Jake tells her. "We're just waiting on confirmation now."

Jolene collapses with tears in her eyes. "No, this can't be true," she moans.

"But it is. I'm sorry for your loss…well, not really, since your husband was a terrible man."

Jolene looks at Tim with a shocked look. "You're a *jerk!*" she yells, and runs off to her room, crying.

"Wow, man," Jake says.

"What?" Tim asks.

"Looks like somebody has been around Jerome too much when he's playing bad cop," Jake replies.

"I guess you're right, but there's no point in lying to that woman—she knows what a jerk her husband is. Let's go see what the guys have found, especially on those computers," Tim says.

He and Jake head toward the master bedroom.

Meanwhile, Jerome and Sheila pull up at the morgue. "I hate coming here," Jerome says.

"So do I," replies Sheila.

They walk into the building and down a long hallway, and when they get to the end, Jerome opens a door that leads to the doctor's office.

"After you," Jerome says.

"Uh, thanks," Sheila says, puzzled.

Jerome smiles at her. "Hey, I'm being a perfect gentleman here," he says.

Sheila looks at Jerome skeptically. "Well, that could be it, or maybe you're just scared one of the bodies will come back to life and eat you, and you want me to check it out first," she says.

Jerome smiles broadly at Sheila and asks, "What would make you believe something like that?"

"Oh, come on, Jerome, everyone knows you only open the door for girls you want to have sex with. And since you see me as a friend, I would assume you must be thinking about all those horror movies you've been watching."

"Oh come on, Sheila I would never use you as a shield," he says. "I have more respect for you than that. I mean after all, you are my friend from childhood."

Sheila nods hesitantly, still unsure of his reasoning.

"I'm glad to see you've come around to believing that I can be a nice guy to a woman without expecting something in return." Jerome pauses at the door. "By the way, I was wondering something about you."

"What?" Sheila asks curiously.

"I know you're disappointed that you got stuck with me and didn't get to go with Mark."

Sheila stares at Jerome. "What? You're crazy. I'm glad I got to go with you; besides, Mark is married, and…"

"So, I was right—you are in love with Mark."

"What? Jerome, how could you say something like that?" Sheila replies nervously.

"You've been acting kind of strange around him. Like you did when you had that crush on him…"

Sheila tries to interrupt him, but he won't let her. "And I saw it in your eyes," he finishes.

"Saw what?" Sheila asks.

"Hope," Jerome says.

"Hope? Jerome, you're crazy!"

"Who are you kidding? I know when you heard Bullseye was back, you were thinking that maybe Debbie might hook up with him again, and then you could make a move for Mark."

Sheila shakes her head. "I gave up on that a long time ago."

Jerome smiles slyly. "Of course you did; isn't that why you are trying to be so helpful with Sonya?"

"Don't be ridiculous," Sheila says.

"Okay," Jerome says sarcastically.

"Okay, indeed," comes a man's voice, sounding like it was spoken with a mouthful of food. Jerome and Sheila both turn their heads toward the door of Doc's office. They see Doc standing there, leaning on the side of the doorway arch, eating a sandwich and looking at them.

"What? Don't give me that look; you two were talking loud enough to wake the dead," Doc says.

"Yeah, Doc, but it was a private conversation," Sheila replies.

Doc leans toward Jerome and Sheila and whispers, "Well, then maybe you two need to learn how to whisper like this."

Jerome laughs. "Okay, Doc."

Sheila laughs as well and apologizes.

"Well, you two were having such a wonderful conversation about being in love with Mark, let me add to the mix," Doc says.

"No, Doc, don't," Jerome interjects.

"Come on, Jerome, she has to know," Doc says. Sheila looks at him curiously.

"Doc!" Jerome says firmly.

"Don't worry, I've got this. A long time ago…well, let me take that back…last month," Doc begins.

"Doc, please," Jerome pleads. "You're going to…"

"Go ahead, Doc," Sheila interrupts.

Jerome is getting more and more concerned. Doc continues from where he left off. "As I was saying, last month, Jerome confessed his love for Mark to me."

Sheila's eyes get big as she looks at Jerome. "You are in love with Mark? Now it all makes sense," she says jokingly.

"Doc, Sheila, quit playing around," he snaps, getting angry.

"Sorry, Jerome, you know I can't make up a lie that quick on the fly," Doc says. "And since I had already said Mark's name, I had to say something."

"I understand that, but did you have to say I was in love with him?" Jerome asks.

"It distracted her didn't it? While she was distracted, I could ask you if it would be all right to tell her about that time."

"So that is what you were trying to—"

Sheila interrupts Jerome. "What time?"

Jerome says, "I don't know if you should hear this. Do you still think—"

"What time?" she repeats. Jerome ignores her. "Please, Jerome, I can handle it."

Jerome takes a deep breath and nods at Doc, who then says, "First, let me clear up something, before Jerome kills me. Jerome is not gay; he likes girls."

"I know that already; I was just joking earlier. Everybody knows he's straight. I mean, after all, I…" Sheila catches herself.

She is thinking about the night she was going to the showers. She remembers heading down, believing that she was on her wayto the ladies showers, but when she saw the urinals, she realized she was in the men's showers. Sheila was relieved that nobody was present to witness her mistake. She was about to leave when she heard Jerome's voice. Sheila sneaked over to see what he was saying. Jerome was alone, looking in the mirror, flexing his muscles and talking to himself.

"All right, tonight is the night that Tiffany is going to be screaming your name. Once she has been with this, no other man will satisfy her." Then Jerome started to laugh. "Oh yes. You, my man, are a sex God." Then Jerome started flexing some more in the mirror. Sheila had to put her hand over her mouth to keep from busting out in laughter. Sheila wondered what Tiffany, another fellow officer at the precinct would have thought if she knew her boyfriend was saying such stupid stuff.

She'd put it out of her mind and got out of there before any of the other male officers could come in and see her. *After all,* she thought, *I don't want to traumatize Jerome; he won't be able to perform.* Once again, she'd had to hold her hand over her mouth to keep from laughing and left before she was caught.

"Sheila?" Jerome says.

Sheila snaps out of her daydream. "Hmmm?" she says and then quickly adds, "We should get back to business. Doc, you were saying something about Mark."

Doc nods. "Okay. When Mark was over here last month, he was talking about you while he was investigating the death of one of Mickey's men."

"Really?" Sheila asks.

"Yeah," Doc replies.

"Are you sure you want to hear this, Sheila?" Jerome asks.

"I know that you're probably right, Jerome. I shouldn't, but I have to know about this. I have to know if I was right about Mark's feelings for me. Besides, this isn't going to change the situation if he tells us now or in two minutes. Come on, Jerome, live a little. And it's good to have something positive come out of this whole situation."

Jerome agrees with Sheila, although in his mind he knows it's just slowing them down in the investigation. But he also knows this information should cheer her up a little. Sheila has been heartbroken ever since Mark and Debbie got married. Jerome has always been there to help cheer her up, but he wonders if she isn't setting herself up to be heartbroken if Mark and Debbie don't break up now that Bullseye is back.

"Mark was talking about what a great girl you are and everything," he says.

"I see; he probably thinks of me as a great coworker."

Doc and Jerome look at each other as if to say, *She doesn't get it.*

Doc replies, "Sure. Whatever you want to believe."

Sheila frowns at him. "Is there more to the story?"

"Yeah, there is more. You know, Jerome really is a good friend."

Sheila looks at Jerome. Doc tells her how Jerome had asked Mark if he would make a move on Sheila if he and Debbie ever broke up.

Sheila is shocked and happy at the same time. "So what did he say?"

"He said yes, he would," Doc answers.

Sheila can't speak; she is just standing there in shock. "Jerome, why didn't you tell me?" she finally asks.

"Because I didn't want you to think that he was leaving his wife for you. You know they are talking about starting a family."

"Yeah, but—"

Jerome interrupts. "Let's get back to work, Doc," he says.

Doc tells them to step inside his office, which is filled with dusty books and furniture.

"Please have a seat," hesays. Jerome asks Doc what he has for them. Doc tells Jerome and Sheila that one of the corpses is definitely Mickey. Jerome and Sheila breathe a sigh of relief at the news.

"Is there anything else?" Jerome asks.

Doc shakes his head. "No. But I do have an interesting story about decapitation."

Jerome and Sheila look at each other. "Well, that is great," Sheila says,"but we have to get back to the station. Right, Jerome?"

"Yeah, that's right. Let's get out of here. I mean, let's get going."

"Aww, come on, guys, why don't you stay awhile and talk?" Doc asks.

Sheila and Jerome get up nervously and head toward the door. "We would love to, believe me, but we have to report back to the captain," Jerome says.

Doc looks hopeful. "Well, maybe next time?"

Sheila says, "Yeah, maybe next time."

They leave Doc's office, close the door, and look at each other. Jerome whispers to Sheila, "Doc gives me the creeps sometimes."

Sheila whispers back, "Me, too."

They hurry down the hallway to the door that leads outside and go out.

* * *

Back at Mickey's house, Tim asks the guys if they have found anything. So far they have nothing. Jake tells Tim the computer guys are still checking both computers; they found some encrypted files that need to be looked at. Tim tells Jake to tell the computer guys to check Sonya's computer.

"Why?" Jake asks.

"There might be something on it that explains why he wanted to kill her."

Jake leaves to go tell the computer guys. After an hour, Tim and Jake meet in the foyer.

"Well, did you finally get anything?" Tim asks.

"Yes," Jake answers. "Come with me."

They walk together toward Sonya's room. "I can tell you, on both Mickey's and Jolene's computers, we were able to find evidence that Mickey was setting up Kiss-Up to take the fall."

"Oh, really? The guys and I haven't been able to find anything else in the house that could help show the gang's activities. Did you find anything in Sonya's room?"

Jake grins and leads him to Sonya's room. "Let's just say that I found fool's gold in Mickey's and Jolene's room. And in Sonya's room, I found the real gold."

They enter Sonya's room. It is nice, with red and black bed sheets on a single bed and a computer on a wooden desk, with a computer chair. She also has a nice, 20-inch TV, a small window with blinds, and a bookshelf with lots of books on it. Tim can see two computer experts Dwayne and Samson sitting on Sonya's bed, inspecting her laptop. The guys show Tim what they've found. It's a video of Mickey being called by his alias name, as well as a file showing all of the drug shipments Mickey has received over the years.

Tim thinks that's it, but then the computer geeks and Jake show him something else, which they think is the real reason he wanted Sonya killed. On the video, they can see Mickey acting gay. He calls his wife by the name of one of his henchmen, Money.

Tim's eyes open wide with this revelation. It's clear now that Mickey has been sleeping with Money. "I see. Well, now we know. If his men saw this, they would overthrow him. I guess none of his men knows that he likes to play both sides of the coin, if you know what I mean."

Jake and Dwayne and Samson agree.

"Yeah," Jake says. "I mean here it is, Mickey, a tough guy—at least that's how he portrays himself but underneath it all he's like that."

Tim and Jake come to the conclusion that Mickey was worried that if this got out, it would discredit him. So rather than having his reputation ruined, he would get rid of the problem by killing Sonya.

Tim turns to the computer experts. "Why didn't he just take her computer?"

Dwayne tells Tim that he gets the impression that she has a lot of copies and that they are probably hidden somewhere. He thinks maybe Mickey thought it would be easier to kill her and eliminate the problem at the source.

"I see what you're saying," Tim says. "He thought by killing her he would be covering all of his bases. I still think what he tried to do is dumb, but Mickey had always been the kind of guy that would kill you first and ask questions later."

Jake and Dwayne and Samson all look at each other and nod in agreement, that this is truly how Mickey operated. That is why no one had ever betrayed Mickey until now. Tim tells Jake to call the captain and tell him what they have found, while he goes and tells the men to start wrapping things up.

<u>SAVE HER</u>

Meanwhile, Mark arrives at the hospital. He walks into Sonya's room, only to find Eric inside, talking with her. Sonya and Eric notice Mark.

"Well, time for me to go," Eric says. He stands up, tells Sonya goodbye, and leaves.

Mark asks Sonya if she knows who is lined up to take Mickey's place when he dies. "Well, it's supposed to be his wife and kids," Sonya says.

"You don't believe that they will be in charge?" Mark asks.

"No. I believe Crazy will over throw them and take control of the empire," Sonya says.

"Can he do that?" Mark asks.

"Yes. Crazy is in good with everybody. They respect him more than they did Mickey," Sonya replies.

Mark is shocked. "Do you think Mickey had any idea?"

"I think he suspected someone, but I don't think Crazy was even on his radar," she replies. Mark ponders what Sonya said, and they begin discussing more about Crazy.

* * *

Over at Mickey's house, Jake is walking to his car and gets in. Tim is already in the passenger seat, waiting on Jake.

"All right, man. Are you ready to go?" Tim asks.

"Yeah, let's go to the station," Jake says, turning on the car. But Tim asks him to take him to the hospital instead. Jake asks why, and Tim gives an excuse about checking on Mark. Jake looks at Tim skeptically. "I know you're full of it. I know why you are going to that hospital, and we both know it has nothing to do with Mark."

Tim smiles broadly. "So are you going to take me?"

"Yeah, I'll take you, but please be careful, man. She's Crazy's girl—if I've got my facts straight."   "I will."

Jake shakes his head and starts driving toward the hospital.

* * *

In the hospital room, Mark and Sonya are still talking.

"So basically, would you say, now that Mickey is dead, that Crazy will be the one to take over?" Mark asks. Sonya says yes, she believes so. Mark asks why she is with a guy like Crazy.

"Well, I guess I should start at the beginning," Sonya says. Her eyes tear up a little; Mark hands her a tissue, and she thanks him. "Crazy has two brothers, a younger one you know as Cleaner and an older brother, Lance."

Mark is surprised to hear this information, because none of the informants ever mentioned this. "I knew about the younger brother, but I didn't know about the older one. Please, go on," he says.

"Well, it was two years after I arrived that I met the boys. They could see that I was still upset over my mother's death, and none of Mickey's other kids would play with me. Lance and his brothers would play treasure hunters, tag, hide and seek—you know, kids' games. They really made me feel comfortable about being there," she says.

Sonya tells Mark how she and Lance became really close and that they were in love.

"But you guys were kids," Mark says.

"I know, but we just bonded anyway. Lance gave me this locket the night we kissed," she says.

"I see why you're attached to it, but if you are in love with Lance, why are you with Crazy?"

Sonya tells him that Lance is dead. A light bulb goes off in Mark's head. *Maybe this is why none of the informants gave us information about Lance.* Mark asks if she knows how he died. She tells him she found out from Gossip that Mickey had Lance killed, and that Lance's brothers did the killing while Mickey took her and the rest of the family out of town.

"After I found that out, I wanted to get revenge, but of course I was too young. So I've been waiting patiently. I've just been collecting evidence against Mickey, and as for Lance's brothers, Crazy and Cleaner, I've been waiting for the right time to deal with them," Sonya says.

"Why has it taken you this long to get back at his brothers?" Mark asks.

Sonya sighs. "I've made a horrible discovery. The problem is bigger and harder than I thought. I can't trust anybody in there except Eric, and he has problems of his own to deal with."

"I'm sorry," Mark says.

"Me too," says Tim, as he walks into the room.

Mark turns and looks at Tim. "How long have you been there?"

"Long enough," Tim replies. He walks over to Mark and Sonya. She yawns.

"I'm feeling kind of tired," she says.

"You should rest. Mark will return tomorrow to see you. Don't worry about anything; everything will be fine," Tim says. He looks at the locket around Sonya's neck and picks it up. "Nice locket. I can see you have taken good care of it."

Sonya looks at Tim, a little confused, and thanks him. They stare at each other for a minute, then Mark says, "Tim, we had better get going."

Tim and Sonya say goodbye to each other, and Tim tells Mark he will wait for him outside. Mark says his goodbyes to Sonya and then leaves as well. Mark meets Tim outside the room, and they leave the hospital together. Tim tells Mark he needs a ride, and Mark agrees to give him one. While driving, Mark tells Tim, "I know Sonya and I are not related by blood, but she is my sister."

"Of course," Tim replies.

"Good, I'm glad you understand, because if you hurt her, I will kill you."

Tim smiles nervously at Mark. "Message received."

Mark and Tim finally arrive at the police station and see Jake, Jerome, and Sheila standing outside, talking. Mark and Tim park the car and walk over to them.

"What's going on?" Mark says.

"Oh, nothing," Jerome replies. At that moment, Jerome looks over and sees Tiffany walking by. She waves at Jerome, and Sheila turns away and giggles.

"Are you okay, Sheila?" Jake asks.

"Yeah, I'm fine," she replies.

"So that was really Mickey's body?" Tim asks.

"Yep, that guy is definitely roasted. Doc checked everything, so you don't have to worry. He won't be coming back," Jerome replies.

"I've told the captain what's going on so far, and he'll call Bullseye and tell him. Make sure, Mark, that you let the captain know what you've found out," Jake says.

"Okay, I'll go do that right now. I need to give him my report anyway," Mark replies.

He is about to leave when Sheila stops him and asks if he will tell her what happened at the hospital. He tells her that he will when he returns from talking to the captain.

"Okay, I'll be right here when you get back," Sheila says cheerfully. Mark smiles and walks into the police station. Tim, Jerome, and Jake are looking at Shelia with big grins on their faces when she turns around and looks at them. "Okay, guys, that's enough," she says.

Tim, Jerome, and Jake just laugh.

When Mark gets inside he goes to Dwayne and Samson's office, he asks them if they found anything on Gina's phone.

"Yeah. Some guy named RJ," the expert replies.

That must be the records clerk guy at the IA, Mark thinks. He asks the guys if Gina had anything else on her phone.

"Yes, she had his address in her phone. I'll give it to you." Samson writes down RJ's address and hands it to Mark. He thanks him and leaves to go to RJ's place.

He arrives at the apartment building and goes up the stairs to knock on the door. No one answers. Mark knocks again, and when no one answers yet again Mark draws out his gun and turns the door handle. The door is unlocked, and Mark enters the apartment cautiously. Upon entering the apartment, Mark can see that the TV is on, but no one is in the living room.

He makes his way to the kitchen, which is clear. He then makes his way down to the only bedroom in the apartment. No one is there when he enters. He checks under the bed and the closet; all is clear.

Then, all of the sudden, he starts to hear water coming from the bathroom. It sounds like water spilling onto the floor. Mark makes his way into the bathroom carefully where he sees water spilling out of the tub. He reaches over to shut off the water and sees, at the bottom of the tub, a man's body that has been tied up and gagged.

"This must be RJ," Mark says. He can see a needle off to the side of the toilet and puts together the horrible events that must have taken place.

They must have drugged him, tied him up, and put him in the tub. Then they ran the water and let him drown. *Poor guy.* Mark examines the tub closer. When the water got high enough it had muffled the sound of the water running.

"They must have done this to try and cover up the time of death, "he says.

Mark takes RJ's vitals just to be sure, and confirms what he already knew—that RJ was dead. Mark calls the station, and when the officers arrive, he gives his statement.

Doc, the Medical examiner, walks up to Mark. "Any special instructions?" he asks.

"Yeah, can you confirm for me how he died, and also if this is RJ from the IA's record department?" Mark says.

"All right. I'll call you as soon as I have the info," Doc replies.

"Great. I'll be heading back to the station for now."

Before Mark can get out the door, however, he bumps into Todd, who is coming in. Mark wonders why Todd is here. He shouldn't have arrived so fast, and why is it only him and no one else from Internal Affairs?

Mark thinks Todd is involved somehow, but he decides to pretend like all is well so he doesn't alert him that he is suspicious.

"Do you need to talk to me?" Mark asks.

"No, you may go," Todd replies.

"Okay," Mark says and continues on his way to the station. When he arrives, he parks Tim's car and heads to the computer experts.

"Something wrong, Mark?" Samson says.

"Yeah. I still can't believe Mickey would want to kill Sonya over some video of him acting gay. There has to be more to it than that," Mark replies.

"That is what we all thought, too. Jeff told us to go over everything again. Here," he says as he hands Mark a box with papers, photos, keys, and cell phones. "Maybe you might see something we missed. You can use that office over there."

Mark takes the box and goes into the other office and starts looking over everything. Mark is feeling more confident because of all the information he has now. He's got a new perspective on this—after all, he seems to be a target now for these guys, though he doesn't know why.

Mark starts looking through all the pictures carefully. *It's got to be something that Sonya and I both have.* Mark calls over to Dwayne and Samson and tells them to bring him all the files he has been putting together to get information on Sonya and Mickey. The guys come back and put the boxes on the table, then go back to their office. Mark continues going through the boxes of Sonya's pictures. He isn't seeing anything out of the ordinary until he gets to this one picture of Mickey and his family on a picnic.

In the picture, he can see the back of a guy with blond hair, but not the man's face. "Hmm, that picture looks familiar to me, like I've seen it before," he says.

Mark goes over to his boxes of evidence and starts looking through the pictures. Then he spots the picture he's looking for. It was almost the same as Sonya's, except it was shot from a different angle. They both have a *Fun Day* banner in the background. Now he can see the guy. Mark's heart drops when he sees it is Todd, the IA agent.

Mark wonders how he could have missed it. He holds up both pictures side by side and can tell they are from the same picnic. In one picture, he can't see Mickey and his family, but you can see Todd being friendly with some of the family. In Sonya's picture, he can see Mickey's family being friendly with Todd. So this just shows that they were definitely at the same place. He decides to go talk with Sonya to see if she can confirm the acquaintance and if she knows anything about Todd.

Mark goes to see if his car is safe to drive. It's not ready yet, so he gets the keys to Dwayne's car, and then heads to the hospital. Mark arrives and goes to Sonya's room, where she is reading in bed. Sonya looks up. "Hi," she says.

"Hi," Mark replies.

"What's going on?" she asks.

"Oh, nothing much. I just thought I would check on you, and ask you some questions."

"Well, I'm doing great, and what do you want to ask me?" Sonya asks.

"You said that you were trying to take Crazy down, but that it was harder then you thought it would be. What did you mean by that?"

"I have some pictures and video showing Mickey and Crazy managing some of the drug shipment," Sonya says.

"That's great!" Mark replies.

"Yeah, but it's not enough according to Eric."

"Really?" Mark asks.

"Yeah," she says. "Mickey and Crazy are the kind of guys that have back up plans for people to take the blame for them without their knowledge. Eric said I needed something bigger."

"So did you ever find your something bigger?" Mark says.

"Yeah, I did. It could take down Mickey and Crazy…well, now just Crazy."

"What is it?" Mark asks.

"That they have a man that helps arrange everything, and makes sure that any cops that start sniffing around are eliminated," Sonya says.

"Are you sure?" asks Mark.

"Oh yes, I was hiding in the air vent when Mickey and his men were having a meeting. He talked about a cop named Cliff getting too close and that he needed to be dealt with along with some informant named Manny."

Mark's heart sank. "Oh my God! Do you know the name of the guy Mickey and Crazy would use?" Mark asks.

"No, but I know he's in big with the police," Sonya answers.

Mark pulls the picture from his inner jacket pocket. "I got this from among your pictures on the computer, and if this is the guy you're talking about, it could explain why you were up for elimination."

Mark shows the picture to Sonya. "That's him!" she exclaims. "Do you know who he is?"

"Yes, that's—"

"Todd from Internal Affairs," Todd says as he moves forward in the room, pointing a gun at Mark and Sonya. "Forgive the intrusion. You two seemed so engrossed in your conversation. So I thought I'd let myself in."

"Where are the guards?" Mark asks.

"I sent them away. I told them you two were going for a walk and they should go eat lunch until you return. So why don't you get out of that bed and let's go take that walk," Todd says.

"I don't think I'm supposed to move around like that," Sonya says.

"Don't worry, it won't bother you for long," Todd replies.

"I take it you're going to kill us?" Mark asks.

"You, yes, but for her, if I do that I'll get a death sentence from someone scarier than me. Now move!" Todd says. Mark helps Sonya to her feet.

They leave the hospital room and head to the elevator. Todd keeps the gun hidden, but still pointed at Mark and Sonya. They enter the elevator and take it all the way to the roof top. They walk off and look down over the side of the building.

"It's a long way down I know, but it will look more believable if I kill you both this way," Todd says as he gives them a sinister smile.

"Wait! I thought you couldn't kill her or else you'd be killed," Mark says.

"True, but if I make it look like an accident, I can get rid of the thorns in my side at the same time. It's nothing personal—that's just the way the cookie crumbles sometimes." Todd cocks the gun and points it at Mark.

"Wait!" Mark cries. "I have some questions before I die."

"What is it?" Todd asks. Mark squeezes Sonya's hand, then lets go and starts to walk toward Todd slowly.

"I'd like to know why you killed Gina, RJ, and Mickey," Mark says.

Todd watches Mark cautiously. "Good question. I killed Gina and RJ because they discovered my secret. That's also why Cliff and Manny had to go, but Mickey…I never took him out."

"Do you know who did?" Mark asks.

"Yes, I do and it's the reason why I'm staging Sonya's death. This guy is pretty dangerous. Mickey has always been afraid of him," Todd says.

"Who is he?" Mark asks.

"Sorry, not enough time to answer," Todd says. But just before Todd pulls the trigger, Mark tackles him.

They fall to the ground and the gun is knocked out of his hand. They struggle and end up rolling to the edge of the roof. They both make it to their feet before Todd punches Mark in the face. Mark hits him back, and Todd loses his balance. He falls off the edge, but he manages to grab the ledge.

"Help me up!" Todd says.

"I will, but only so you can face justice," Mark replies.

"Face justice," Todd scoffs. "Oh yes, our wonderful court system. I'll be out soon for good behavior and then I'll make sure I finish what I started for you two."

"You're right. A guy like you will never change," Mark says. He begins to loosen his grip on Todd's arm.

"What are you doing?!" Todd screams. "You can't do this— you're one of the good ones. You can't be bad. What about all the information I know?"

"I'll figure it out, but this is the only way Sonya and I can be safe from you. God forgive me," Mark says as he lets go of Todd's arm.

Todd screams as he falls onto the metal fence on the floor below, his body impaling on the sharp, spear-like edges. Definitely dead.

Hospital staff runs outside towards Todd's body, and when they look up to try to see what has happened, they see Mark.

Sonya walks up to Mark and grabs his hand. "You did the right thing. Don't feel bad about it."

"I crossed a line that I never should have crossed," Mark replies.

"I know, but you saved more than both of our lives today. I have no doubt that there were others on his hit list," Sonya says.

"I know you're right, but I still took a life," Mark says.

"Is this the first time you've killed somebody?" Sonya asks.

"Yes," he answers. "I'll tell them everything. I can't ask you to keep such a secret."

"Mark, even though we're not blood, we're family. You're all that I have. Family always sticks together. I will never abandon you. And I will keep your secret of what really happened to Todd. No one needs to know that you let him die on purpose. I won't lose you," Sonya says.

"I won't lose you either, little sister," Mark says.

Mark and Sonya hug, and as they do they can hear the police sirens coming toward the hospital. The other cops make their way onto the roof and take Mark's and Sonya's statements about what happened. Sonya is taken back to her hospital room while Mark goes to the station with Jerome.

"Don't worry about that Dwayne's car," he tells Mark. "I'm letting Jake drive that back to the station. I thought with everything that has happened you don't need to be driving now. You might still be in shock."

"Thanks, man," Mark says.

"Tell me something, Mark. I know this is off subject, but do you still feel uneasy about Jake?"

"Not anymore. I use to think that he was still trying to get Debbie back, but the captain helped me to see that he isn't interested in anyone but Cindy. I guess I was being paranoid since Bullseye always seems to be trying to get Debbie back," Mark says.

"Well, I'm glad you see that. Why don't you get some rest before we arrive at the station? You've got twenty minutes, then you can go and give the captain a full report," Jerome says.

"Thanks," Mark says and then closes his eyes and goes to sleep.

Jerome wakes up Mark once they arrive at the station. They go inside and Jerome heads to his desk while Mark heads up to Jeff's office.

"So, Mickey had an IA guy," Jeff says."No wonder we could never get him on any of the drugs or bank robbery crimes. Heck, even the extortion case we couldn't get enough evidence against him."

"I know. I'm sure Todd had a hand in making sure anything that could implicate Mickey disappeared," Mark says.

"I'm sure you're right," Jeff replies.

"I'll just go and fill out the paperwork about what happened at the hospital," Mark says.

"All right, good job," Jeff replies.

Mark heads to his desk.

"Do you need a hand with your paperwork?" asks Sheila.

"Sure, that would be great," Mark said.

Jerome, Jake, and Tim stop by Mark's desk before leaving for the day. "Hey Mark, you need anything before I go?" Jerome asks.

"No, I'm fine. Sheila's helping me with the paperwork, so I'll be able to leave soon."

"All right man, stay safe. See you tomorrow," Jerome says as he leaves to go home.

"Well, I'm glad to hear you're okay," Jake says.

"Thanks," says Mark.

Jake leaves and Tim is the last one hanging around Mark's desk.

"What's up, Tim?"

"Well, I figured since you're so busy with this paperwork, I'd better go by the hospital and check on Sonya for you," Tim says.

Mark laughs. "All right man, whatever. I know you like her. Tim, you don't have to try to make something up. You're a good guy. Go ahead, you have my blessing."

"Thanks," Tim replies, smiling big as he leaves.

Mark looks at Sheila. "Thanks again for staying and helping me."

Sheila smiles just as big as Tim had. "No problem," she says.

Something Unexpected

The phone is ringing inside Bullseye's house. His house is average looking, with the usual furniture, but everything is covered in dust and the plants are dead since he had been undercover the last two years. Bullseye runs from the bathroom to answer the phone. He is still dripping wet from the shower and trying to wrap the towel around his waist as he picks up. "Hello?"

"Hey, Bullseye," Jeff says on the other end. "How is it going so far?"

Bullseye tells Jeff that everything is fine so far.

"Good—and by the way, Mickey got blown up. I thought I would just let you know."

Bullseye is shocked to hear it. "Wow! I guess we'll be having a meeting tomorrow morning, then?"

"Yes, at 8:00 sharp. See you there."

"Yes, sir," Bullseye says and then hangs up the phone.

He's walking toward his bedroom when he hears his doorbell ring. He walks over and looks out the peephole. To his surprise, he sees Debbie standing at the door.

Debbie can hear some muffled sounds coming from the other side of the door. "Bullseye? Is that you?"

"Yes," Bullseye responds calmly.

"May I come in? We need to talk," she says.

Bullseye opens the door to let her in. She sees Bullseye in a towel and smiles at him as she walks inside. He closes the door behind her, and after, everything feels eerily calm, like the quiet before a storm.

In the peaceful, middle-class neighborhood where Bullseye lives, the residents are in their homes or out for an evening walk; all is quiet on the street. But on the hillside overlooking the neighborhood, there are several figures looking down at Bullseye's house: Crazy, Killer, Money, and Informer. They see everything that just happened with Debbie and Bullseye. They look at each other and then back at the house.

Informer turns to Crazy. "Well, I told you this is where the rat is. What do you want to do with him?"

Crazy has an evil smile on his face as he looks at Bullseye house intensely. "Time for us to take out the trash," he says.

"And what about the woman?" asks Killer.

"Well, it's not our fault she decided to come over to his house at this time," Crazy replies.

"I'll call the other guys and tell them to get over here right away. We've got business to take care of," Informer says.

"Yes, you do that," Crazy says. "I can't wait to hear what Bullseye has to say."

Crazy laughs psychotically as he stares at Bullseye's house.

THE END